KORAKAS

Anne Holloway

Big White Shed

To Charlie
Thank you for all your
support over the years
as a proper friend
to do xo

Published by Big White Shed, Nottingham, England
ISBN 978-0-9933805-0-1
Printed and bound in Great Britain by Clay Ltd, St Ives plc

Hope you enjoy this
much love
Anne
x

For
Sarah Williams.

With thanks to
Jo Rowland, Jack Rowland and Luc Haynes-Holloway
for patience and tireless interest.

What's the worst thing about having a crazy mother? Probably the underlying, nagging concern that one day she will flip out and disappear.

What's the best thing? The highs which more than make up for the times when I have to coax her back out of the low spots. The laughter. The stories. The fairy-tales.

The child opened her eyes and spoke, "tell me again, where I was born." She lay on the bed, one arm thrown up above her head and across the pillow, as if she were resting on soft grass, eyes wide open. Anna knew if she spoke softly now, she could whisper her daughter to sleep, so she answered.

"You were born on an island at the farthest reach of the Mediterranean, where snow tips the mountains and the sun shines, the sea laps gently at the shore, where the golden sand is tinged pink by tiny crushed shells. Crystal clear water runs down the mountains and cascades into lakes to provide water for the islanders. The food is plentiful, with olive groves and orange groves, lemon trees outside the window. Scented flowers to perfume the air at night, to send you off to sleep."

She stroked her daughter's hair, pushing it back from her face, waiting for the next demand.

"And tell me then, why we left?"

And so began the fairytale.

There was a Dark King who had stolen the land from his forefathers. In the summer he allowed his people to be warm and happy, they wanted for nothing, but in the winter he would bring down terrible storms to show his might and keep them from disobeying him. But in stealing the island he brought upon himself a terrible curse, he became trapped. So although he ruled as king he was very unhappy and lonely. Now there was a girl on the island, who came from a far-off land. When the people saw her, they fell under her spell.

- Oh! How beautiful she is! A precious girl! A Princess! Skin as white as the snow on the tops of the mountains, eyes like dark roasted almonds, hair as golden as the sand on the beaches.

Now the King knew how much the people loved her and he knew that if he held her captive they would obey him for fear he would harm her. But he grew to love her and believed that through love he could break the curse, be free once more and rule with her at his side. But the people feared his plans for the girl and vowed to help her escape, even though they would be left to suffer at his hands.

The child was asleep, her breathing hardly audible, her hair plastered to her head sticky with sweat. She burned hot at night. Her eyelids fluttered slightly, half open. She slept with eyes half open too, just like her father did. Her mother flicked back the curtain to check the window latch was tightly shut and peered out into the darkness, where the trees shifted. Satisfied that all was quiet, she drew the curtains tightly together and left the room, careful to leave the door ajar.

Just as her daughter was soothed by the familiar tale, for Anna it reawakened memories.

I burned the coffee this morning. He hates that. He didn't speak but I see his face tighten, his mouth turn down, hardening his features. He was out late last night and he's gone to meet someone today about 'business'. I'm so nervous. Ally is playing outside in the yard and I'm trying to leave everything as if we have just walked down to the village.

I put her favourite toy on the floor by the television, a cup of milk half-drunk, a biscuit on a plate. I hear the chickens squawking, then footsteps outside. The birds scatter as Karen thunders into the courtyard, leaping the ones which get in her way.

"I've left the car round the back, where's the luggage?" She is breathless and distracted.

"In the apothiki," I point to the door of the storehouse on my right.

Andy arrives from the flower farm, where he works in between his bouts of drinking.

"Alright Anna?" He grins showing an array of crooked teeth. He seems sober enough today. He helps Karen carry our cases to her car down a track behind the house. She turns and waves. I wish we could travel with her, but she says we would be too conspicuous driving away in her tiny car with suitcases crammed in the back.

"See you there," she calls.

I raise my hand in reply as she speeds off down the track. I turn to Andy. He's forcing his lips into a smile and touches my shoulder tentatively.

"I'm not as daft as I seem, or as drunk as you think." He hands me a grubby carrier bag. "Go put these on." I look inside and find black clothes, a village widow's outfit.

"Look Ally! Mummy's playing dressing up." I slip the old dress over my head, shawl around my shoulders and cover my hair

10

with the scarf. I leave the back door open, as we usually do when we're close by.

With Ally on my hip, I follow Andy around the edge of the property towards his farm, turning to take one final look at the house I have called my home for nearly three years. Andy is loping along and I have to run to keep up with him. We reach the farm via a tree-lined track and skirt round the poly-tunnels bursting with gerberas. Their colours don't suit this landscape, they're outsiders, like me. Behind one of the outbuildings is a motorbike. I'm still wary after all these years but I know that I have to get on.

"Don't worry," says Andy, " I'm safe when I'm sober."

I hold Ally to me, her legs round my waist, and bind her close with the shawl. Once we are on the bike you wouldn't know there was a child with us at all. Andy stinks of earth and stale sweat, but I hold him tightly.

He takes a side road towards town and onto the Ethniki briefly before cutting off again and we make our way on the back roads, through the villages. We stop a couple of times. It's a long trip on a bike. I realise this may be the last time I will drive through olive groves and see goats ambling across the road. Ally is quiet, as if she knows something is happening, maybe she is lulled by the motion of the motorbike and the closeness of me.

When we reach the airport on the other side of the island, we pull into a lay-by. Andy is so tall, as I hug him round the waist my face is buried in his chest and I can't help inhaling that odour, but I'm so grateful that I don't want to pull away.

"Thank you."

I walk, shifting Ally onto my hip again. We cross to the airport and join the throngs of tourists on their way home. I feel safer here, anonymous. Karen is waiting at check-in and hands me the tickets. She hugs us as tight as she can.

"The flight leaves in an hour. Go straight through to departure. Change at Schiphol, then on to London."

"Thanks," is all I can say before she runs off again.

We stand, Ally and I, in a queue of happy, normal people, with two suitcases to our name.

The flight from the mainland had been more like a bus ride and took less than an hour. I arrived at a small airport, with little security. Outside stood a row of taxis, their drivers leaning idly against them, unimpressed by the arrival of the last few passengers. It was late evening and I felt cold. I wondered if I should have brought more clothes and pulled my scarf closer in to my neck. It had survived the tumble dryer but had lost that special smell it had when I first wore it. As I walked towards the row of cars, one of the drivers, chewing on a toothpick, asked where I wanted to go. I realised I had no idea. All the stories had been about trees and mountains, no names of people or places.

"Town please, the harbour," I told him and held my bag out to him confidently. One thing my mother had taught me, never show fear or apprehension. The driver took my bag and threw it into the boot, then opened the passenger door for me. I hesitated but chose to get into the back of the car, and as we sped off down the track I was glad that I had. He drove in the centre of the road, flinging the car around each bend, turning to smile at me like a fairground lad on the waltzers.

I hardly took in the view of mountains on one side and coastline on the other, as we dropped towards the town. The streets were unfamiliar. I had hoped that somehow I had filed a memory to draw on. The driver tried to make conversation, chewing on the toothpick, glancing in the rear view mirror. "Where you from? English?"

I grunted replies and he soon gave up. We drove past a tree-lined square and turned down a narrow road flanked by shops and restaurants. There were T-shirts and handbags hanging outside for sale, postcards and gifts. I noticed a large church on my right, in a square, then the taxi stopped at a chain strung across the entrance to the harbour. He could drive no further, but would have to turn again and skirt around the harbour, back up to the main street.

"Which hotel?" He asked.

"This is fine. How much?" He asked for twenty Euros, a bit much, I thought, but paid anyway. He flipped a lever to open the boot of the car, glanced in the mirror, then got out slowly and walked round to hand me the bag. He stood watching as I stepped over the low-slung chain. I heard him suck air around the toothpick and was conscious of my walk as he watched me.

"Creep," I muttered and felt better. I had seen this view so many times in pictures, books, brochures and on the internet, longed to see where I was born. I had planned trips here for years. Almost booking flights, pricing up hotels and apartments, but never having the courage to ask my mother to go with me. She would never have agreed. Either side of me were restaurants and bars, with rows of seats and huge umbrellas. In front of me was the harbour, sweeping around in a semi circle, an ancient lighthouse at the far end of the wall. I knew there was a small hotel on the harbourfront, painted blue with balconies overlooking the waterfront. I had seen it online and imagined staying there with mum, the two of us sitting on the balcony watching the world go by. I thought I would check in there until I found something more permanent. As I scanned the buildings, I found the hotel, paint faded now, but still recognisable.

The only room available was tucked away at the back, reached by an alleyway parallel to the harbour front. It might have been a storeroom at some time. It had a separate door with a window on one side. I opened the door and climbed the few stone steps inside. There was a kitchen area on the right, with a stove and a tiny sink, even a fridge under the worktop. On the left of the stairs were two single beds with a chair between them, a low table in front of the window and cupboards built into the wall. Straight ahead was a door leading to a bathroom. The receptionist had apologised and promised to let me know as soon as a better room became available. But having seen it, I thought it would do fine, preferring the stillness of the back street to the bustle of the waterfront.

I've always been afraid of the dark. But here I am in a strange place, the village tucked up for the night, walking to the beach. The tourists love beach parties and we often walk down to show them the way. Hot balmy nights, cheap booze and a dodgy DJ playing crappy pop for girls in sarongs and silver sandals, dancing their best for some waiter with a smattering of English. But tonight, I walk alone. The lights from the village fade behind me and I feel my way along the path, a footstep at a time. Although the grasses rustle, I concentrate on banishing all thoughts from my head, except how to keep going, controlling my heartbeat, and stepping forward.

I can hear the sea, and as I walk farther from the village towards it, I can just pick up the sound of music and a faint glow of lights strung around the beach bar.

"Brave, walking alone in the dark," I swing round, my heart swollen to twice its normal size inside my chest, and I will it not to beat. I'm not so afraid once I can see it is a man and not some mythological monster from beneath the sand dunes.

"Bloody idiot, you scared me to death." He laughs. I try to place his accent.

"You're English?" I guess.

"Spend time with the English."

"That's not much of an answer."

"Not much of a question." He falls into step alongside me, guiding me by the elbow as we walk. I hide my resentment as I'm finding it hard to feel my way in the dark and he appears to have no problem whatsoever.

The bar comes into view in a pool of coloured light. A small crowd is gathered, dancing and chatting on the sand, a mix of local boys and tourists.

"I'll get you a drink."

I hesitate.

"Don't worry! No strings! I'm not one of them!" He... again. I suppose he's attractive, bit too old maybe, anyway, too of himself. I nod to the barman and ask quietly,

"Who is he?"

"Anna, I don't know everybody!" He throws a sideways look at the man and moves quickly away to clear some glasses.

I'd kept myself 'clean' while I'd been here. No sleeping with waiters or bar owners, no throwing up after heavy drinking sessions, just working and swimming and lying in the sun, watching the antics of the rest of the world.

"That Anna is such a clean girl, for a foreigner," I heard one of them whisper to another as they swept their front steps one morning. If I was offered a ride on a motorbike I declined. An offer of a lift from a man on a motorbike was often an opportunity for him to show off his latest conquest. I had learned some lessons from watching the other's mistakes. If a girl accepted a drink, she was saying 'yes'. I said 'no'. Tourist girls committed crimes against the moral code without even knowing it. I, on the other hand, kept my secrets. If I had adventures they were private and with people who shared the same set of rules as me. This is a crazy place with crazy people in it. Smiles on the surface and prejudice buried beneath.

"So? What'll it be?" He persists. The barman winks at me.

"Anna only trusts labels, scared we serve bomba and she'll get ill! And she's right, drink what the boss drinks and you'll be safe, not the cheap stuff we sell to that lot." He jerks his head towards a group of girls slinging shots of a green liquor down their throats.

"Then I shall drink what Anna drinks."

"Okay, and next time I'll buy for you."

"Next time?" He looks suddenly out to sea, as if he has heard something, then turns his head towards me with a flashing smile.

"Yes, next time." And he raises his glass to me.

I wanted one of those sticky-sweet black coffees my mother used to make. I tried to keep away from the cafés on the front, where the waiters worked so hard at charming the tourist girls. I'd seen them trying it out on one group and then another at opposite sides of the café. I wanted to sit quietly and watch people, gather my thoughts. I looked across the harbour towards the old lighthouse and scanned round until I spotted a small kafeneon where the locals seemed to meet, on the corner of the harbour and an alley, which ran along the back of the restaurants. The waiter looked up as I walked through the tables, and I chose one about half way back. After a while he ambled up to me and threw back his head slightly, raising his eyebrows. He mumbled something I didn't understand, but I guessed he was asking what I wanted to order.

"Coffee... gliko," I tried out the word I'd learned from my mother for 'sweet'. The man raised an eyebrow and strolled back inside. After a few minutes he returned with the coffee and a glass of water.

The harbour was busy. A family trudged past, children trailing behind their father, while the mother stopped to look at postcards. One of the waiters from the large café on the front was standing chatting to an old guy who had been wheeling a moped towards the chain at the top. A dog sniffed around at the front of the kafeneon where I sat and then ran barking after a big black crow that had settled on a bag of rubbish by the water. It flapped its wings effortlessly and flew away over the rooftops leaving the dog jumping in circles and yelping. The waiter came forward and threw something at it and it ran off.

A woman walked up and sat at one of the tables in front of me. She folded her long limbs under the table as deftly as she unfolded and re-folded her newspaper, creasing back the pages and began filling in a crossword. I strained to see if it was in English. The woman turned slightly to beckon to the waiter and caught me looking at her. She smiled and then stopped. She asked the waiter something and he looked across at me, before walking back inside. I looked away quickly, pretending I hadn't noticed.

"Jesus Christ!" An American voice rang out. I looked to see who had spoken. A round-faced, stocky man was standing next to the woman. They made an odd couple.

"Doug! Sit down." The woman hissed at him as she tugged his arm. She was clearly English, I noted.

"Sit down!" More insistent, she pulled him into a chair next to hers. He kept turning his head to look at me and the woman kept scolding him under her breath.

I finished my coffee and stood up to leave, looking around for the waiter. He came forward from his seat.

"You from England?"

"Yes." I pulled out my purse, but he waved it aside.

"You pay tomorrow," and walked back to his seat.

"But I might not..." I started to say, but the man had gone. As I walked past the couple, I hesitated and stopped to speak to them.

"Excuse me. I wonder.." The woman grabbed for the man's arm, and looked up at me,

"God! It is! Alithea!" Nobody called me Alithea, except mum. Everybody called me Al or Ally. When I heard it spoken like that, I panicked. I ran. Looking back I saw the chubby American puffing behind me.

"Hey, miss! Please! Gimme a break will you?" Shouting for me to stop. I turned up an alleyway, a dead end. What an idiot. He caught up with me.

"You gotta be careful round here. These back streets are tricky. You think you know where you are, but..." he walked towards me, looking anything but menacing, his face red with exertion. He held out my bag, I must have left it at the café. His voice was soft and reassuring.

"Here you go." He offered it to me at arm's length.

"I thought – you were chasing me." It seemed ridiculous spoken out loud.

"Hell hon, those days are over. Come on, walk back with me I'll show you the way."

"Been here long?" He asked casually.

"Just arrived."

"Holiday?"

"Not really. You?"

"We live here."

"I was born here." I heard myself say.

"So it is you. We were pretty sure we were seeing things. But there's no mistaking really! Welcome home." He smiled and gave my hand a squeeze. We had reached the harbour again and I let him tuck my hand under his arm as he led me back to the café.

The woman was sitting, alert at her table, watching for us, looking this way and that. When she spotted us, she lunged out of her seat and ran towards us. She touched my shoulder lightly, ran her fingers down my arm, then taking my hand, walked me back to the table. The American joined us, still breathing heavily and signalled the waiter for service.

"I knew it was you," said the woman. "Where's Anna? Where's your mum?"

I loathe Chrissoula.

"Oh Anna! I'm an old woman," she wails as she lowers herself onto a plastic chair and squeezes her fat backside firmly into it. She lifts a foot to rub it, letting her grubby mule drop to the floor. She crams her feet into shabby flip-flops although she has a cupboard full of fancy shoes at her villa in town.

Poor Chrissoula. She fell in love with Manolis at fifteen and married him, against her family's wishes. She told me how his brothers had stood guard with shotguns outside the church, waiting for her family to turn up and snatch her back. 'I loved her that much!' Manolis would laugh. 'Can you believe that?' I find that very hard to believe. Manolis with his quiet manners and ready laugh, she with her dull wit and sharp tongue. They moved away from the island to start a new life, then returned, funded by an insurance pay-off from an accident at work. She may have lost her looks, the skin on her arms and neck would never recover from the scalding water from a pan of hot water, but their bank account was full. That made up for it. They could buy a business, build a house in town overlooking the bay and drive a nice car. Careful not to spend too much in case the tax-man took a closer look at the books.

She lumbers, no she shuffles, like a patient in a mental home. She's only forty-two. A dumpy, whining piece of work who leaves all the hard graft to me. Like a fool I run around getting everything done. The kitchen chores are the worst - always just one more thing to be done and to be done her way. I slice the tomatoes instead of cutting them in chunks, I cut too much off the okra, my salads are too generous, my portions too large. I sweep the floors the wrong way, pushing the dirt away from me instead of pulling it towards me. As soon as I can, I swap the kitchen tasks with her daughter and volunteer to clean the few rooms she rents to the tourists who stream off the buses every day. I tempt them to come and look at the rooms. Tired and thirsty they accept and invariably stay. Once the rooms are let and the cleaning done I'm free for the day. Free to walk to the beach, to the west of the village where few tourists bathe because the river runs freezing cold from the mountain into the small bay. I love the shock of the cold, heat of the sun, searing sand under foot and a cold blast of water on my skin as I dive in. I lie and watch the ducks venture out from the river into the bay. A peculiar sight, ducks on the sea, a bit like me, a pale skinned English girl at large in this village.

I'm thinking about the man at the bar the other night when the ducks are startled and fly off in fright. A lone crow swoops down and hops to the water's edge. My skin feels cold. Perhaps I've lain too long in the sun. I gather my things together and begin the jump skip across the hot sand to the path which leads back to the village. The way is lined with eucalyptus trees, which cast beautiful shade, but encourage the mosquitoes to hide here, close to the river where they hatch out. This is my favourite time of day. My skin is tight from the salt and heat and sand. The cicadas are deafening, but I am alone as I walk. A dog lies tied up under a tree just past the small hotel on the corner. Two old men outside the kafeneon nod as I pass and return to their game of Tavli, slapping the pieces into place at the roll of the dice. A few tourists sit outside Sunrise Bar nursing cold beers and burned feet.

I pass the periptero and wonder if I should buy Chrissoula her copy of the Ethniki Typos, a rag which has a full colour front page every day, depicting a car crash or burned out house, a man accused of murder, or a girl badly beaten up by a foreigner. She loves to read the stories and suck air through her teeth, tut and mutter, Panayia Mou, Mother of God, over and over shaking her head. She worries about "the aige" taking over the world.

"It's Aids mum – for Christ's sake," her daughter whines in her Antipodean accent every time her mother mispronounces it. They moved back here when she was twelve and she hates it. She can hardly write in her mother tongue and her English isn't that good either, split between two cultures, stuck working for her mother.

20

I am angry with myself for spoiling my quiet time with thoughts of that woman. I feel cold again. Ridiculous.

"So should it be coffee this time?" There he is, as he was the other night. That man again, from nowhere. Taking my elbow he leads me to the corner café and gestures to the old man sitting in the doorway. He pulls out a chair for me to sit and dutifully I do.

"You'll take a coffee with me Anna, yes?" He speaks as if English is not his own tongue, but his accent is perfect.

"I don't like the coffee."

"You will like this. Taste." The old man has returned with two small cups of steaming treacle and mutters something under his breath. An incantation or a blessing? Instantly my companion shoots a stream of words back at the old man which sends him scurrying back to his post at the door. I understood none of it and sit feeling foolish. He lifts one of the cups to my lips.

"Drink," he says, and I do.

I felt sick when I got back to my room. The shutters were closed and I was grateful for the darkness. I'd been desperate to get away from those people. I lay on the bed waiting for the nausea to pass. Maybe I'd had too much sun. I was trying to catalogue events, sorting through it all in my mind. It seemed ridiculous that the first full day on the island I should meet people who knew my mother. Not just that, people who seemed to have been pretty close to her. The woman kept taking my face in her hands and calling me "baby" over and over again. Doug was less forthcoming. He'd written down the name of a taverna.

"We'll be there tomorrow around eight. Join us, please. We can talk." He had walked me to the corner of the street and held me by the elbow, very serious.

"My wife was very close to your mother. Last time she saw you, you were only a baby. She took it badly when you left."

I could hear people walking past the window. They spoke in different languages, some words I understood and some meant nothing at all. A moped fizzed past. A man called out to somebody. I let my mind drift into sleep.

Chrissoula is driving me crazy. I got two bills mixed up last night and some couple have paid less than they should have for a meal. She is raging about it, how hard she works, how little money they have. I've worked nearly three months straight for her now and each time I ask for my wages she moans about how much she does for me, how she treats me like a daughter. She feeds me, she talks to me, she treats me to ice cream when I drive with them up into the hills, late at night when the taverna is closed. If I feel like a prisoner, how does her daughter feel?

The floor is swept, tables ready and chairs in place and Chrissoula sits on her huge arse fanning herself.

"Ahh-nnaa?" She wails and that's it. I can't take any more. I sweep my arm across the table nearest to me, sending napkins, vinegar and oil flying onto the floor. She screams terrified, as if she fears I'll come for her next.

"Enough!" I shriek. "Enough of your whining!" I march shaking to my room at the side of the kitchen and throw my clothes into the holdall I keep behind the door. I return, wielding the key for the door, tears on my face and bag slung across my back.

"Here, take the key. Look!" I brandish it in front of her.

"Let everybody see me give this back to you now. Don't let me hear stories of how I crept back at night and robbed you in your sleep!"

Manolis, her long-suffering husband appears from behind the huge grill area where he prepares all the meat.

"Anna" he speaks softly. "Rey –Anna, pou tha pau? Where will you go?"

But I don't care. He digs in his pocket and as I walk by he thrusts a roll of notes into my hand and squeezes it briefly. Then he shuffles back to his grill to prepare for the evening as usual.

"Oh you bad girl," wails Chrissoula, "what shall I do? It is Maria's Day tomorrow."

The Feast of the Annunciation is a massive holiday. They gorge themselves on seafood in celebration of the Virgin Mary. Let her wait on the lot of them without me.

"Go to the crows then!" She screams at me in a final verbal assault. Manolis rushes towards her and tries to quiet her, but she struggles with him, yelling at me.

"Go then! I've seen you with him! Go!" So I go as she's told me. She's a crazy village woman with her mad oaths and stupid superstitions. Once I am safely away I stop and laugh with relief. How could I have stuck it for so long? Hadn't I come here to escape all of this, to relax and live life for me? I look at the ball of money in my hand and count it out; enough to keep me for a week or so, until I find work away from here. I feel elated. It is dark now, the light has dropped suddenly, and the trees cast strange shadows on the road. I head off for the village square to find myself a room for the night. There are of course raised eyebrows, but they know what she's like. They've seen girls come and go before. They all have a story to tell about her, but they have a story to tell about each and every one of their neighbours, few of them complimentary.

I woke with a start. Someone was knocking at the door. A light, agitated rapping. I sat up on the edge of the bed and touched my head. It felt too heavy for my neck.

"Ally? Alithea?" I recognised the American's voice.

I opened the door a crack to take a look. He seemed harmless enough. As I stepped back to let him in I caught sight of a man leaning on a motorbike in the alleyway. He smiled broadly at me and nodded slightly, unashamed to be caught staring. I felt embarrassed and looked past him up the alley, as if I'd been looking for somebody else and when I looked back again he had gone.

"Doug? Are you alright?" I didn't know him, but I felt suddenly concerned for the man.

"I'm fine. I just wanted to see you." He glanced this way and that as he spoke.

"Please, sit down," I pointed to the other bed and moved to the small kitchen area to boil some water. He remained standing.

"I'll make some coffee." I went through the motions I had watched my mother make, countless times, spooning coffee into the briki, stirring carefully. I loved to watch mum in the kitchen. It was the centre of the house. Making coffee was one of the hangovers from life on the island. Strong, dark coffee, brought slowly to the heat in a briki, a long handled pan which holds just enough for two cups. She used to stir the treacley mixture gently until it rose up into a froth and pulled it from the heat before it boiled over. You must never break the waves Ally, she would tell me as a child, not for the perfect coffee.

"You are so like your mother." Doug sighed.

"I have to find her." I hung my head, the weight of it suddenly too much.

"Find her?"

"Oh! I've broken the waves!" Doug leapt forward and pulled the briki from the heat, burning his hand in the process. I stood, arms at my sides, helpless.

"I don't know where she is." Doug pulled me to him and I leant my head on his shoulder. He smelled clean, like I imagined a dad should and I felt myself relax a little.

"Shh," he said as he patted my back awkwardly.

When I felt sure I could control my voice, I spoke again, explaining the events that had brought me there, alone.

*

One more week to go and I'd be free. Only the obstacle of telling mum was in the way. I walked up the path to the house considering the best way to broach the subject. Me and Rachel had planned to go away for the Summer and Pete had begged us to include him. Besides, taking a boy along would please the parents, they'd presume he'd act as protector to us girls, although given his levels of testosterone, I doubted he'd be much use in a crisis.

Turning through the gate I stopped by the pond in the front garden, remembered years ago how I had woken up in my bedroom to hear the sounds of a spade hitting clay and rock. I pulled back the curtains and looked out onto the garden. It sloped up and away to a fence hidden by shrubs and bushes. Mum was bent over hacking away at the bank in front of the shrubs.

"What are you doing?" I called down to her. She stood up straight and swept the hair away from her face with the back of her hand, that way she does even when there's no hair there. She stood motionless for a moment and I watched her. I struggled to open the window wide to call again, but couldn't ever work those safety catches. So I went downstairs and out into the garden. When mum saw me she beckoned me over.

"Look!" She threw her arms wide like a magician's assistant.

"What are you doing?"

"Building a stream." She struggled on over the weekend and

when it was finished we lay on the grass and imagined we were in a woodland, with a babbling brook playing over the rocks as the water dropped from the top pool to the bottom. I love the sound of water. So does mum.

"If I can't live by the sea," she said, "at least I can lie here and listen to the sound of the stream."

When I was small I would ask her, "why can't we live by the sea?" But I learned to give up on that one. That was one of the things that could spark an episode. The sea is where we felt most happy but it was where mum seemed most afraid. Anyway. There I was standing, remembering, when she saw me.

"You're early," that broke the memories, "thought you'd be late today. French wasn't it? How did it go?"

"Good actually. I was really pleased. Famous last words!"

"Just forget it till you get your results, you've done your best, worked hard." She stroked my hair, "you always do. My girl."

We linked arms and walked inside the house and through to the kitchen, swaying our hips into each other. I'm shorter than mum and curvier. Your grandmother's hips! Mum would tease. When I was little I could never keep up with her, those long strides she takes. But now I can. People say how much we move the same, how we look the same, pale skin and dark blonde hair. I was trying to work out the best way to approach her about this trip.

"Shall I make you coffee?"

"No, I'll do it," she was laughing. She had shown me how to make coffee since I was a little girl, gently bringing it to the boil, watching the froth form on the top and taking it from the heat at the right moment, just before it boils up and over, breaking the surface, the waves. I watched quietly as she went through the familiar process, concentrating, head to one side.

"Mum?" Silence. The gentle hissing of liquid heating and the sound of the spoon catching the sides of the tiny pan she used.

"Me and Rachel were thinking of going on a trip, and Petey might come too, safety in numbers." Mum stirred the coffee, rhythmically.

"Just for a few weeks, till results come out. Take our minds

27

off it." I wasn't sure if she was listening.

"Three's a crowd." She continued stirring. Encouraged by the response, I went on.

"Petey doesn't count! He sort of makes up the other halves of us, he's like an accessory we share!"

"Sure he'd love to hear that. What happens when he decides which one of you girls he fancies?"

"Mum! Petey's as queer as they come." She turned to look at me and did that raised eyebrow thing.

"Is that right?"

"Yeah, that's right." No resistance yet, so I took a breath to continue, but she interrupted.

"And you'll be paying for this trip, how exactly?"

"Well, I'd saved a bit from work and I thought.."

"You thought I'd cough up?"

"Well, if I'm not here, I wouldn't be eating here, so the money you would have spent on food here, I could spend on food there.."

"And where exactly is 'there' Alithea." My full name, always a bad sign. This was the piece of information I was afraid to give up.

"The islands." Mum let out a sound, almost imperceptible above the sound of the coffee rising to the boil, but loud enough for me to know she was upset. She poured the coffee carefully into a cup and carried it over to the table where I sat. Her chair dragged noisily on the floor as she pulled it out from the table. She lifted the coffee to her lips, blew across it, then slurped carefully, to avoid burning her lips. I hate that sound. Why not wait for the stuff to cool before she drank it?

"Well?" I knew I sounded belligerent, I wished I could have held that back, but all the years of avoiding this issue were pressing in on me, willing me to ask the questions.

"Well," mum countered, "you must know how I feel about this?"

"Not really. We never discuss 'THIS'." My father, my birth place, our flight back to England. "I am afraid to discuss THIS," but I checked myself and continued, "because I know it upsets you and I love you." Resuming the role I've become so accustomed to playing, dutiful daughter, sometimes the parent. Mum dropped her head into her hands.

"Please Ally, you don't need to go there. Please. I can't protect you there." I could feel tears on my face, but I wiped them away. I would not cry. I'd seen enough tears during my childhood and I had no desire to add to them. One of us had to keep it together.

"I don't need protection Mum," I knelt by her side and laid my head in her lap. "You've taught me how to be strong, to be careful, to keep out of trouble."

"None of that will matter if you go back there," she whispered.

I could feel it all building up inside, tears filling my eyes. What choice did I have? This is always how it went. This is how it always went her way.

"Don't you see? I'm as trapped here with you as you say I would have been there with him?"

"Come here," she pulled me onto her lap and cuddled me, like I was small again. But even back then I knew that it was more comfort to her than it ever was to me.

"You're right," she said, "but what can I do? I've spent my life keeping you safe. How can I explain how it happens? You don't know what it's like when you're there. The place has a hold on you, makes you act in ways you never thought you would."

I could feel myself slipping away. I'd heard this all before. At first the stories had been about the mountains and the sea, monsters that lurked in the waves, birds that kept watch in the trees, a princess with almond-shaped eyes. Bedtime stories and fairy-tales. Then later they took a darker turn, mum seemed to really believe the fantasy she had woven. Like the time she took against Michael. He was a boyfriend I suppose. Sometimes even now, I still miss him, or at least having somebody like that in our life. I was maybe seven or eight at the time. He used to dance with me, call me Princess Alithea and twirl me up and around till I was dizzy. He even persuaded mum to go to the seaside. Then there was that picnic on the beach.

He tried to get a fire going to cook sausages, but it wouldn't start. So he'd given up and gone to fetch chips, determined we would have a feast at any cost. He had only been gone ten minutes when the light disappeared, the sky darkened on the horizon and the rain fell. Mum gathered up all our things, grabbed me by the hand and we ran like crazy chickens laughing and screaming to the car. As we peered through the steamed up windscreen, we saw this figure zig-zagging across the path in front of us, a carrier bag in one hand and a teapot in the other. Mum flipped on the engine and leaned on the horn. The figure stopped in his tracks, bolted across to us, jumping puddles, mouth flapping open and closed with words we couldn't hear, waving his arms, tea splashing out of the spout of the pot.

As he got closer I could hear heard him shout,

"I went to the chippie! They made us a cuppa!"

He looked like a…

"He looks like a big black bird," I said, delighted, turning to mum. But she sat with her hands on the steering wheel and wasn't laughing anymore. Back at the cottage where we were staying we heard him calling through the letter box,

"What have I done?"

"You don't fool me!" Mum kept calling back, "Go back and tell him it hasn't worked."

"Anna, let me in," pleading with her, "what do you mean? Let me in."

We went home without him. He called the house a few times, even came round, but she would never let him in.

If I think about it, I realise that was when the delusions really began and the stories became darker, stronger, more complex. Sometimes I would play along just to stop her from being upset. If I listened quietly and pretended to believe, heed the advice given, it would stop sooner and we could get back to normal. Now I wonder if that had made it all worse.

"What if I promised not to go to his island?" I smoothed the hair from mum's face and held my hands there for a moment, like she'd do to me. "What if we went to the islands, but not his?" She didn't answer, so I went on. "He can't cross the sea right? So he can't get me as long as I'm not on his island."

I could feel her body relax beneath me and when she spoke she seemed calm.

"You're right. I'm keeping you captive. I'm sorry. I sound crazy. Forget it. I am crazy. You go, but not to his island, that would be alright wouldn't it? Besides, you've seen one island, you've seen them all, right?"

**

The wind is slipping through the trees again tonight.
It is creeping beneath the hedge and lifting the leaves before it
scuttles down the grass towards the house.
I am clutching a strip of tablets in my hand.
I took them once before.
They stopped the rustling at the edges of my thoughts and I could
focus then on the everyday, getting up, sending Ally to school,
working, eating.
But they make me dull and drain the fight out of me.
"Better to face your fears," I tell Ally.
"Then you know what you're dealing with."
She is brave, not afraid like I am.
I hid that from her when she was a little girl.
Now she's older she knows I am afraid but she knows I challenge it.
I will put these tablets in this drawer, right at the back.
If Ally finds them she'll be angry.
That time I took them before she said it was like I had been taken
away from her and she was left with another woman.
"Promise," she said, "promise you won't leave me, promise
you won't take these," and she had flung them on the floor at my
feet.
When I asked for help back there, they believed me.
When I ask for help here they give me pills.
But my lovely Ally doesn't believe, she trusts that I want the best
for her, but I know she doesn't believe me.

31

**

We had planned to meet up for lunch at the restaurant where I work part-time. Richard, the owner, well he's a friend too, he had put on a spread for me.

"For you, because I love you like my own baby," he said, and kept pinching my cheek.

"Where's Anna?"

Mum was always invited, she's as much part of the group as I am. Then she swept through the door almost colliding with a waiter, who sidestepped and blushed and she apologised.

"Here she is." I called her over to join us. She looked great. I mean, everybody says how much we look alike, but I wonder if I'll look that good when I'm her age. She's tall and 'slender,' no lumps and bumps and she walks like a young woman. There are streaks of grey in her hair, but that makes her seem more exotic somehow. She hugged me and kissed me on the cheek as if we'd been parted for days.

"Sit here," everyone squidged up to make room for her on the bench seat. The table was strewn with wrapping paper and half empty wine glasses.

"We started without you, sorry."

"Here, have some wine." I stretched across the table and picked up the carafe and mum held out a glass as she carried on chatting to the girls. She put it to her lips and drank, then stopped, bringing the glass to the table with a bang.

"What d'you think?" Asked Richard. "You know I always listen to you."

I think I was the only one who sensed a change in her mood. I looked across at Richard as he waited for her response like an eager puppy waiting for a treat. He's single, younger than mum, but definitely has a thing about her. I mean I can't see anything wrong in a woman dating a younger man.

"Where did you get this?" She asked him, waving the glass at him.

32

"It's a sample from a new supplier."

"Tastes like village wine," she spat the words. The wine coated the side of the glass. It was dark, almost brown.

"I like it," I chipped in, trying to lighten the mood.

"How much have you had?" Mum snapped.

"Hey! I'm eighteen now, remember?" I tried to sound light. It was often something small which set her off, and she seemed precariously close since talk of the trip.

"Here," Richard replaced the glass and refilled it from a fresh bottle.

"Oh Richard, thank you." She was fine again. "I'd ditch that stuff before it makes someone ill."

"Look at all this stuff they've given me." I tried to change the subject and began to unwrap the parcels piled in front of me. I came to a parcel from Richard and unfolded a bracelet. I held it up to the light, so the sun could catch the tiny glass beads, all different shades of blue, suspended from these irregular rings, which form the links. I wear it all the time now.

"It reminded me of that ring you always wear on the chain round your neck." My hand flew involuntarily to my chest where I wear a silver ring on a long chain.

"It's a kind of love ring I think, Mum's got the other half." As I spoke I could see mum twisting the ring on her finger.

"Look, they fit together," I pulled out my silver one from under my shirt and held it next to mum's. Hers is gold, with a tinge of pink to it.

"So they do," Richard peered closely at them, "looks like yours should have another ring on the other side,"

"There is no other ring," Mum snapped again.

"Open mine," Rachel pushed a box across the table, trying to change the mood. Maybe she was used to Mum's way's too and knew how to switch her. Rachel had given me an alarm clock with two massive bells on the top.

"Very funny."

"For when you start Uni. We know what you're like in the morning."

"If I get into Uni."

"Oh here we go! You're bound to get in," I looked up to see lanky Petey behind her.

"Petey! You came."

"Wouldn't miss your birthday bash, especially with the delicious Richard hosting," he winked at Richard and the poor man stammered something before disappearing back into the kitchen.

"Who gave you this?" Mum was holding up a scarf, I wear that all the time now too! It's woven from some kind of long fibre, very soft. I can't make out if it's green or black. It's so dark and it kind of shimmers, has a sort of lustre to it. I picked it up and threw it around my shoulders.

"Richard said some customer left it for me. Isn't it gorgeous?" I remember pulling it up to my face and nestling into it, breathing the scent deeply.

"It smells like.."

"Christmas," Mum finished for me.

"What? Yes it does. Cold air." And it did. Fresh and cold, like a blast of air from outside. The kind that lingers around someone as they come in stamping their feet to get warm. I looked at my mother. She seemed frozen in her seat and suddenly looked her age.

"Mum, are you ok?"

"Yes of course." Bright again.

**

I heard a noise.
Everything seems in its place as I walk through the hallway and into the kitchen.
I retrace my steps and open the front door.
Nobody.
Those bloody birds watch from the beech trees.
As I close the door I notice a feather on the doorstep and I bend to pick it up.
Signs to confuse me, like the wine and the gift.
I thought I'd done everything I could to keep Ally from harm.

Should I step back and let her go now?
I run upstairs to find the box with the other feathers.
Some are like down and others are strong like quills.
They have a beauty I must admit.
I close the lid and carry the box downstairs to the kitchen.
How many hours have I watched Ally in this kitchen?
Sitting at the table drawing, rolling out pastry, helping me make
my coffee, climbing into my lap at night when I used to sit and cry.
Her presents are heaped on the table.
That scarf is wrapped in white tissue paper.
I pull it towards me and unfold the layers.
It's so soft.
I lift it to my face and breathe in the familiar scent.
Sharp cold fills my lungs.
I must get rid of this.
I carry the scarf and my feathers into the garden and drop them
onto the rickety barbecue we built in the corner.

**

We usually leave the back door unlocked, so I walked around the side of the house to get in. I can never be bothered to dig my key out of my bag, it's huge bag and everything gets lost in there. The door was wide open, and as I came up the path I could hear my mother inside, opening and closing cupboard doors.

"What you looking for?" I asked her, as casually as I could. I made her jump though.

"Bloody idiot! You scared me."

"Sorry." I noticed her glance out of the door, past me, so I looked too. The garden, shrubs, path, then I noticed something heaped onto the old barbecue.

With forced brightness she said, "make me some coffee, last chance to get it right!" But I strode to the barbecue, knowing what was on it, my scarf. I pulled it out off and as I did I knocked an old cardboard box, spilling the feathers which had been inside it onto the ground. I picked one up and walked back towards the house.

"Ally," she was pleading with me.

"Mum, please." I dropped my head, defeated. Then looked up at her. She patted the chair next to her, summoning me to sit, so I did. I leant forward and wiped a tear from her cheek and she leant forward and wiped one from mine, then whispered,

"What a pair we are. "

"What are you doing, mum?" She had no reply.

"Is it okay for me to go?" She pushed back her chair and pulled me onto her lap. Comfort.

"Ally. Koukla mou! Of course you can go. I was burning those stupid feathers. The scarf, was on the table, it got mixed in. Look, it's the same colour." Her hands shook as she held the scarf up next to the feather. It was the same colour and had the same sheen.

"So it is," I said, not convinced about her confusion. "What are you doing with those feathers anyway?"

"Oh, I collected them, you know, for our story. But I don't need them anymore."

"So why burn them?"

"Because they're enchanted feathers and must be destroyed or the King of the Ravens will come and get you!" She held her hands up like claws and bared her teeth at me. That made me laugh. I thought I'd let it go, but rescue my scarf.

"Yeah right! Now I know you're fine. Just leave my scarf alone." I slung it around my neck and one shoulder raised, gave her a screen siren look.

"I think it's to die for, darling!" Mum smiled and lowered herself into the chair at the table again.

"Go ahead, burn those mankey feathers. Make a spell," I told her.

**

The kitchen is empty without Ally.
I try to imagine how she is spending her days.
At least they never flew to the islands, took a cheap flight to the mainland.

36

*They will be eating the food, drinking the wine, soaking up the
sun, it's all the same to them. Island, or mainland.
She'll be safe.
It is a test for me, to see how far I can let her go and still feel her
close to me.
She will come to no harm.
SHE WILL COME TO NO HARM.
I say it aloud, to the house, to the trees where the birds sit.
I hear that noise again at the front door.
I get up to take a look, open the door to catch a glimpse through
the hedge, of a van driving off.
Inside the porch is a package.
It has the address but no name on it.
I turn it over to see where it is from, some kind of promotional
thing?
I close the door and wander back into the kitchen with it.
I think I'll make a coffee first.
One large spoonful of coffee, sugar, water and bring it slowly to the
boil on the gas until it rises into a perfect froth.
Take it off the heat and pour it into a cup.
What a creature of habit I have become.
I pull the package to me and tear off the wrapping.
Inside is a light wooden box, like our old dominoes box.
I slide off the lid and pull away some coloured shredded paper
inside.
Underneath lies a small bottle and a punnet of fruit.
I look to see if there is some kind of card, but find nothing. I know
what's in the bottle, but even so I open the stopper and breathe in.
Rich, sweet, wine.
The fruit I recognise too, they are despilas.
Tiny yellow plums from the island.*

**

And the trip? It had been a disaster, from start to finish. I felt angry
and guilty. Angry at Rachel and Pete, angry at mum for flipping

out like that, guilty that I had gone to the one place she had always been afraid of. This was bound to happen, but I had so desperately wanted to be like a normal girl, like all my friends at school, not having to second guess my mother's moods, or deal with the fall out afterwards.

The train was packed and I had to stand most of the way. I leant against the side and rocked with it. I pulled the black scarf I'd got for my birthday up to my cheeks and sniffed it. The smell was as strong as when I first wore it. I closed my eyes and tried to relax. When we got to the station, the rain was lashing down. It hit the dry streets and ran in torrents down the gutters. I was soaked from the knees down, the rain trickled off the bottom of my coat and my jeans absorbed it all like they were made out of blotting paper. My feet were wet through. I had to stand all the way on the bus too and jumped off at the corner of our road. The path to the front door was flooded and I jump-skipped to avoid the worst of the puddles. I knew where the dips and potholes were. I walked around the house to the back door, expecting it to be open, as usual, but it was locked. I dropped to my knees to rummage in my bag for the front door key. As I did something sharp poked into my knee. It was a feather, long and dark. The trees round here were full of crows, big noisy black things my mother shouted at to go away.

I found the key and ran back round to the front of the house, slipping and sliding in the mud, anxious, because we never locked up like this. The house was quiet. I dropped my bag on the floor and flung my dripping coat over the end of the banister.

"Mum?" I kicked off my wet shoes and pushed my feet into a pair of slippers from the pile of shoes by the front door. Calling again as I walked into the kitchen,

"Mu – mmy!" It used to make her smile when I called her Mummy. She liked it. I looked across to the window and saw that one of the panes of glass was shattered, there was blood on it. The kitchen was a mess, as if someone had swept everything off the table in a rage. My mother had that kind of temper. When she blew, she went wild. I was calm though, taking in the scene, trying to record every detail. I bent to pick up some broken glass, a small tumbler. It

38

was sticky and glued up my fingers. I sniffed. Like sherry. The floor was covered in papers and bits of glass, a broken coffee cup and coffee grounds and something sticky squashed underfoot.

I stood a chair the right way up and sat on it, hesitated for a moment, then reached for the phone in its cradle on the dresser. I began to punch out nine, nine... and then set the phone down again. Both the front and back door were locked, there was no sign of anyone breaking in. This mess was the sort of thing Mum did when she felt hemmed in, shouting, 'I'm sick of it all', then swinging her arm across the table sending everything flying. Afterwards she would clear it all up and apologise.

'*I feel so powerless Ally*,' she said once. What would I tell the police if I called them?

I tried to imagine what might have happened. Piecing together the details I could see. From the state of the window it looked like a bird had flown into it and frightened her. Normally I would be there to calm her down. I should have told somebody about her. I had called the house several times from the airport, with no answer. I told her I was on my way home. I promised her I was on my way. I started to feel angry, upset. Why couldn't she wait, sit tight and wait? I was certain there was nobody in the house, but still I hesitated at going upstairs alone. So I reached for the phone again and flipped open the battered book we keep all the numbers in, always beside the phone, scanning the entries, I stopped at Richard's number and called him. He didn't ask much. I said very little. Just asked him to come. Then I sat at the table, looking down at my hands and waited quietly.

**

He has ways of reaching me.
He casts spells. He has envoys.
He always knows where to find me, wherever I am.
His breath can draw me in across oceans.
Running away was the wrong thing to do, like running from a
bullet. Run towards it, run towards it and you can seize control.

"Ally, are you in there?" Richard was banging on the door. I leant on the table, feeling suddenly tired, and pushed myself to my feet.

"Yes, coming," I called back. I flicked on the lights as I walked through to the hall. It was getting dark outside. I opened the door to him, and he hugged me, a little awkward.

"Thank goodness you're safe, I can't believe those two just left you out there on your own." I shrugged.
"Well, it wasn't quite like that." He followed me through the hall and into the kitchen.

"God Ally, what a mess. Shall we look upstairs?"

"I already have. She's not there."

"Ally, the whole point was that you wait for me."

"I know, but I knew nobody was there." We climbed the stairs together and I opened each door to show him inside. In Mum's room, one of the drawers on the chest was slightly open, but everything else was neat and ordered. I felt sick, and that made me want to lash out at someone.

"At last you made it to my mother's room!"

"Ally, really." Richard's face flushed. I shouldn't have said that.

"Come on, we all know you have a thing for her."

"I'm fond of you both, but you know your mother is so – different and so – serene." He paused before choosing each word.

"Serene? My mother? Have you seen the mess she's made downstairs?"

"Why would she do that?" Deflated, I sat on the edge of the bed and patted the space beside me. How could I begin to explain what my mother was really like, to him? He saw her public face, the bright and capable woman, who worked at the huge bookstore in town, raised her daughter alone with no visible signs of help from friends or family. *Ally is my whole family*, she would say. Some of her paintings gave her away, the dark ones, the bird ones. She would paint them after an episode, as if a bout of depression gave her clarity. All she could accomplish when she was at her lowest, was to travel to the shop and go through the motions of cataloguing and restocking, advising on 3 for 2 offers and the latest travel journals.

"My mother has always been troubled."

"Are you telling me your mother's mad?" He turned to look at me and I felt colour rush to my face. Ashamed of how I was behaving, ashamed of keeping a lot of stuff quiet for years and ashamed of divulging family secrets, letting her down.

"No, just that she had a tough time of it when I was little and sometimes it's like it comes back to haunt her."

"So what exactly happened?"

"I don't know really. She's so independent. I don't suppose the average islander could handle that."

"I can't imagine Anna with anyone average," he said more to himself than me. "What was your dad like?"

"You know Richard, I don't know." I couldn't stop the irritation in my voice.

"She must have told you something, shown you pictures," he probed.

"No pictures, no details. Just.."

"Just what?"

"Stupid fairy stories."

"You never asked about your own father?" He was incredulous. A lot of men had asked me who had been lucky enough to capture someone like my amazing and perfect mother. She never seemed the least bit interested in any of them. Some had asked what kind of man could produce a daughter like me, but I was never interested in them either. In that too, I am so like my mother.

"That's right. I never asked. If he mattered she would tell me, we'd still be there. If we needed him, we would be with him."

"But you must want to know?"

"Not if telling me hurts her!"

"But he…"

"Let it go Richard! She is the only person I need to know about, she's my whole family, remember? And right now I don't know where she is!" He got up and held his hand out to me.

"Sorry. Let's make a few calls."

"Calls?" I ignored his hand. I didn't want to feel touch right now.

"Find out where she's got to."

"I need to clear up first."

Richard followed me back downstairs to the kitchen. I filled a bucket with hot water and squirted in some detergent, like I was doing routine cleaning. Not that I do routine cleaning at home. But like a proper cleaner, you know? Quiet and methodical. Our feet were sticking to the floor and he pulled up first one, then the other.

"What's this sticky stuff?"

"Some kind of fruit, I'm not sure. Looks a bit like plum." I waved a broken tumbler at him, I felt a bit lighter, "wine too, and her so snooty about that stuff you had at yours the other day." He sniffed it, then stuck his finger in the residue.

"Mmm, tastes a bit like it, too." He sat on the table, his legs swinging while I mopped the floor.

"So a bird hits the window, cracks the glass, leaves a smear of blood. Your mum freaks out a bit because she hates birds."

"She doesn't hate birds, just those rooks in the trees."

"Crows," he corrected me.

"Rooks, crows, ravens, all the same to me."

"She's locked the doors, it's not like she's panicked. Maybe she's simply gone away for a bit."

"She knew I was coming home."

"So you spoke to her. What happened then? I've had Pete and Rachel's garbled version."

"It just wasn't what I expected. Mum was right."

"Go on."

"She said three's a crowd and I laughed. I thought Pete, well we all thought didn't we? I thought we'd explore together. Rachel was a nightmare, a few drinks and she was all over the place and Pete loved it." I put the mop down and crouched to pick up some pieces of broken glass.

"We'd go to the beach, then have lunch in this caff. They'd

42

get stuck into cocktails and I'd sit and play backgammon, Tavli they call it, with this old guy. He told me stories about the village, about the islands, who invaded here, who died there, massacres and battles." I carried on mopping, the same piece of floor over again, slapping it first one way, then the other as I carried on talking.

"All Pete and Rache wanted to do was get hammered, it was pathetic. I get that from Mum."

"You get a lot from your mum," he said it quietly, and reached out to stop me mopping and held my hand. I felt the colour rise to my face again. But this was different. I had always felt Richard was my mum's, you know, interested in her. Now I felt confused. I mean, he's younger than her, but I never thought that mattered. Of course he's older than me, but not that much really. Anyway. I was confused.

"She hates drunks." He dropped his hand quickly and looked away. So I carried on to try and shake it off, that awkwardness I mean.

"So one day, I don't know which, it's only been a week, but I feel like we were there for ever. Anyway, I get back from the beach, go into our room and find the two of them at it. I just felt, I mean why bother going away with me, we were supposed to be mates." I carried on slapping the mop up and down across the floor.

"Then Pete has the nerve to tap me for a loan, and Rachel goes and gets my mobile nicked because she's chatting up some dodgy character outside a sleazy bar. Even Pete got the hump about that."

"They said you were staying out there?" I stopped and leant on the mop.

"I was going to go to the island. Just take a look."

"I see," he shook his head, "but you came back home instead?"

"This old guy was telling me about the island, he knows everything, like a proper historian. So I told him about me, where I was born, how we'd left when I was little. How I wanted to go and take a look but my mum was scared for me. I was laughing about it, telling him some of her stories about clockwork crows and birds in

43

trees, and he says don't I know anything about Daedalus and how he invented strange mechanical things, like clockwork crows and wicker bulls, the labyrinth?"

"Oh I know about the labyrinth"

"Yeah I know about the labyrinth too, but he went on and on and said I should respect my mother and she was wise and I should listen to her and go to her. He frightened me, he started jabbering away and I couldn't understand the words. His son came out and had to calm him down and told me he was sorry, his dad got like this sometimes and I laughed because I said my mum did too – but then I thought, he's right, respect your mum, call her, talk to her, do as she asks. So I called her from a hotel in the square."

"And when was this?"

"The day before yesterday."

"And? What did she say? Had this happened?" He flung his arm out to take in the kitchen. " Ally, how was she? What did she say?"

I tried to remember exactly what we'd said to each other. Mum had been upset, frightened, she'd hit a black spot. I realised that I had to get back to her. I had thought of calling Richard but I didn't want to involve him. I could tell Mum had been crying, but was trying to hide it from me.

- He knows where you are, he's sending for you. I'm coming to get you.

- No mum, I'm coming back, it's okay.

- It's too late for that. I knew this would happen. He needs you baby, he can't let you go.

- I'm coming home, I can change my ticket, fly back tomorrow.

- I'll go to him, I'll persuade him. Don't come here now, he's sent charms.

- I'll be there, hold on please.

- I'll beg him to let you go.

- Mum. Please wait for me. Can you do that?

"Ally, how did she sound?" Richard was insistent

"She was upset. I told her I'd come home." My mind was racing now. Talking to him like this was helping put it all into order. How could I tell him everything, anymore than I could talk to the Police? How could I explain the stories and the fantasies, what was real and what wasn't? I didn't know that myself and to find out I couldn't have him clouding the issue. I needed time to sort through what I knew and what I had guessed at. So, I thought quickly.

"D'you know, she might have gone to stay with Michael in Wales."

"Michael?" He looked hurt. Poor Richard. So it was Mum he was interested in.

"He's just an old friend of her family, we used to visit when I was little," I was astonished how easy it was to lie all of a sudden.

"We used to go when she was feeling low, he was like a grandfather to me," the lies kept coming.

"So call him." I forgot for a minute, what he was talking about. I looked blank.

" The chap in Wales."

"I don't know the number, it might be in her book," I glanced across at the battered notebook by the phone, playing for time.

"Is he very old?" He went on.

"What?"

"Well not such a good idea to call an old chap too late, that's all."

"You're right," Richard you're so practical, I flung my arms round his neck and felt him flinch slightly. That rush to my face again. What was going on here? I looked quickly up at him and smiled to try and make light of it, "sorry," I'd clearly embarrassed him. He glanced at his watch.

"You go," I said.

"It's just we've got a party booking in tonight."

"Of course." I closed the door behind him and sat on the bottom stair. My coat had dripped onto the stair carpet and now I was wet again. I realised my hair was hanging in rat's tails and my jeans were still steamy from the soaking they'd got in the rain. I needed to change. Upstairs I rifled through drawers, realising I didn't have many clothes, they were still screwed up in my bag from the trip, shoved into the dirty laundry basket waiting to be washed, or lying crumpled on the bedroom floor. I ran the shower until it was steaming hot, peeled off the soggy layers and stepped in. I stood with my head thrown back, the water washing over my face. My thoughts were drowned out by the sound of the water. I opened and closed my mouth and sucked in some of the water then let it spurt out again like I used to as a child at the swimming baths playing the Kraken game with Mum. We used to take turns at being the sea monster chasing each other.

The only home Mum had was here with me, or the island. When she used to tell me stories about it her eyes would shine and then flash as she remembered something painful. She would look away and change the subject, or make a joke.

I patted myself dry and wrapped the towel round me tightly. I am roughly the same size as Mum, and we do swap clothes sometimes. The drawer which had been left half open had a few jumpers in it. I needed a pair of trousers. I opened the drawer below and poked around in it. One by one I searched the drawers and realised that certain clothes were missing. The dark grey trousers Mum wore to death, that felted sweater she said was her favourite, even though it was going through at the elbows. I checked the wardrobe and noted the missing items, her suede pumps, the cotton jacket, a couple of dresses, a skirt.

She's gone. I said it out loud. The tears began to fall, like I never let them, as I stood alone, clutching a towel to me, in my mother's bedroom.

Why have you left me?

**

Shh baby girl. Skin as white as the snow on the tops of the mountains, eyes like dark roasted almonds, hair as golden as the sand on the beaches. I will rock you to sleep.
Tell you tales to keep you safe.

Those birds in the trees woke me early. I had a stiff neck from sleeping at an odd angle on my mother's bed. I looked around the room and had an overwhelming sense of being alone. I would have to make careful plans. It was clear to me now that if my mother was not here in our home there was only one other place she could possibly be. She had been gabbling on the phone about going to him and pleading with him and hadn't listened to me asking her to wait. I bundled up my damp clothes from the bathroom floor and took them downstairs to chuck into the washing machine. As I pressed the start button the machine began to turn the clothes around.

"Oh shit," I noticed my new scarf was tumbling round with my jeans and thought, "that'll be ruined." I flicked on the kettle and picked up the telephone.

"Hello, Richard?" I wasn't in the habit of lying and felt guilty about last night, but I needed to put his mind at rest. He was a worrier and I didn't want him to make a fuss.

"I'm fine. Feeling a bit foolish actually. I don't know what came over me." He began to disagree, but I cut in.

"I'm going down to Wales today, once my clothes have dried out. I'll call you from there. And Richard, you won't tell anyone about this will you? I'd rather keep it between us. Mum's very private, we both are. "

I felt a bit smug at being such a convincing liar. I'd never tried it before. I rummaged through the laundry pile to see if there was anything suitable to take with me and ran down the stairs to stuff the few items into the top of the bag I'd dumped inside the front door last night. Then I went to the kitchen to make a list. We are great list makers, mum and I.

Always prepare my mother had told me incessantly. Assemble your tools first, that way you are ready. I found a pad of paper on the windowsill and turned to hunt for a pen in the drawer of the kitchen table. My hand rested on a packet and I pulled it out to take a look. Tablets, my mother's, her name and date of birth clearly printed on the label. The date of dispensing was quite old, but the tablets were still in date. I opened the packet and started to read the leaflet to find out what they were, although I thought I already knew. Years ago I insisted she throw something like these away. They seemed to steal her essence. I love her vibrant and alive, even if that includes the odd moment of pot throwing and yelling. I wondered if she had been taking these, if she might still be here with me.

I'd blown my birthday money on the stupid trip with Pete and Rachel, but I still had the money I'd been saving for driving lessons and the credit card Mum had thrust into my hand before she went away, "strictly for emergencies." Good job I'd never mentioned it to the others. I'd need to get a flight booked. I hoped I could get one closer to home, so I wouldn't have to traipse all the way back to Gatwick.

The washing machine had come to a halt and I transferred my clothes to the drier, first untangling my scarf from around the leg of my jeans. Ruined. The fibres had matted together. I tossed it into the drier hoping it might fluff back into shape with a bit of heat.

*

Doug sat quietly as I spoke, trying to follow my garbled tale, twisting and turning, jumping from present to past and from one memory to the next.

"She raised me on fairy tales, and now I am afraid for her. I think she believes them."

"Ally, honey. Your mother was always very, emotional, very susceptible to feelings and your father had great strength."

"You knew him?" I was excited.

"I met him. None us really got to know him." He looked to the door and back again. "He was strong, physically and mentally. He had power here on the island. Few people crossed him."

"Is he still here? I mean is he here now?" I grabbed his hand tightly, like I could squeeze the memories out of him. Someone who knew my dad and might actually be prepared to talk about him, answer the questions I'd kept locked down for so long. He laughed and pulled his hand away angrily.

"Is he here now? It's like he's always here. Your mother was right to fear your father and she did right to take you away from him!" He touched my hand again, lightly. "That man couldn't harm you back in England. He would never come after you, but here? You shouldn't be here! We worked so hard to get you away and now you're back!"

"Please don't shout at me." I held my hands up to my cheeks to try and stop the tears. I was damned if I would cry in front of this man. I would not cry. There'd been enough tears from my mum for me to add to them. "Please. I just wanted to find her. She said she would come here." He seemed defeated, and I felt sorry for him. He leaned forward and stroked my hair, then looked towards the window and sighed again.

So here I am in town. I'll get the rest of my stuff some time. I have only been here once or twice before. I feel like a villager, fresh in on the bus. I realise how little I understand, I've been learning a bizarre form of the language from a woman who speaks half English, half her mother tongue. I can order food and drink, name a few household items, that's about it. I've learned a village dialect and bits of slang and I'm not sure if any of it can be used in regular company. I am suddenly homesick and wish I could call home and talk about everyday things, the old, every day things. I have a sudden urge to be amongst my own people. I remember an English-run restaurant from my last visit here. I follow the flow out of the bus station and across the busy main street. Most people drift towards a shop-lined street and I go with them. I walk in the road to avoid them as they stop to gawp at T-shirts printed with slogans, leather sandals and handbags, chess sets, replica knives, jewellery. The road descends towards the harbour. I am propelled by the noise, voices, car horns, motorbikes, shouting, laughing, a multitude of different languages. The street widens into a square with cafés and restaurants on every side. Waiters in tight black trousers and bright white shirts smile and cajole to get me to sit and eat in their place. Some reach for my arm. Life in the village has made me afraid, that woman has taken my confidence. Somewhere in the back streets is that restaurant and if I can find that, I'll be okay. If I turn up here it's somewhere on the left, but the houses rise up on either side, it's hot, I don't recognise the names. Someone takes my elbow and begins to guide me like that night in the village as I walked towards the beach in the dark. I hear a voice warning off the boy waiters as they move to lure a new tourist girl in for lunch. I am angry and pull my arm away.

"Anna, you're lost." Him again. Why is he here? I am lost. I'm lost and they're all grabbing at me. I need him to keep them

away. I don't understand what they're saying. But ahead of me I can see the restaurant and I turn, confident again.

"No. I'm going there." I point. I'm running now, leaving him standing and I weave through the tables outside. I drop into a chair just inside the door of the English place. A woman looks up from her crossword and smiles. I begin to cry.

When Doug left it was getting dark again. The light went so quickly here in the back-streets. I felt confused. When I had pushed Doug for information about my father he clammed up again.

"You'd better speak to my wife about that," is all he would say. We arranged to meet the following evening at the taverna on the other side of the harbour. "And be careful about walking through the back-streets at night. There aren't enough people around to be safe."

I needed to eat. I threw a jacket round my shoulders and tucked my scarf into the pocket. I felt anxious, venturing out, Doug's warnings rattling in my head, turning immediately left and down to the harbourfront. As I passed a doorway something brushed past me and made me jump.

"You should be careful walking in the dark." The voice seemed to come from the shadows. I spun round to see a man holding out my scarf, which must have slipped out of my pocket. I took it from him, our hands touched briefly as he studied my face. I could smell that fresh cold smell again and thought it must be from my scarf. "Oh. Thanks," I said, as nonchalantly as I could. But he had frightened me, and he unsettled me, and there was something annoyingly attractive about him. As he stepped out of the shadows I realised he was the man who had been leaning on the motorbike outside my apartment. He nodded his head slightly and watched as I walked on towards the harbour. I walked slowly and deliberately, aware of every step I took, wanting to get away, but determined not to let him think he'd rattled me.

"Don't run," I thought. "Just keep walking." I hooked the scarf around my neck and realised it smelled of washing powder, not the cold at all.

The girls chat incessantly while we set up for the evening. We take turns with the chores, a real democracy, in stark contrast to the village.

"That guy gives me the creeps."

"I think he's a bit of a dish"

"Dish? Nobody says 'dish' anymore."

"Well he's tall." Alison loves tall men and they are scarce on this island. The girls have marked a place on the wall opposite in the street, which corresponds to her height. If a man walks by and is a head above it they go running to tell her. It's a kind of sport on a quiet night. Finding Al a tall husband.

"Where d'you meet him?" I realise they are asking me. I look around to see who they mean. He's across the street talking with one of the waiters. The boy looks upset, his head down. Looks like he's being told off.

"I don't even know his name."

"He knows yours."

"What do you mean?"

"He often asks after you. I thought you knew him from the village."

I haven't thought about the village for weeks now. I feel rejuvenated. Life here is good. I work, I get paid, I go out. Each night we have an adventure. We watch films at the open-air cinema near the park, a backdrop of a night sky and sounds of traffic adding to the action. Some nights we take a raft across the harbour to a nightclub set into the harbour wall. You can walk round but it's quite dark and the stones are uneven and slippery in places. Tonight after work, we go to the Bazouki. We double up on mopeds and bikes and drive out in a group. The club is off the main highway, at the foot of the mountains. The boys order bottles of whisky and vodka, which are slammed on the table with a handful of glasses, no mixers. They pay for everything, it's their way. There's some headline act playing, they're mad about her.

"Checkout the big hair," Alison whispers to me. Not to mention shoulder pads, gold shoes and floral prints. Truculent, gum-chewing girls walk in between the tables selling rose petals on tin foil plates, which cost a day's wages. These are thrown at the chanteuse to show appreciation of her talent. A man on our left calls over a waiter and hands him a wad of notes. The waiter disappears and returns with six bottles of champagne. He stands on stage next to the singer and opens one after the other, pours a glass from one of them and hands it to her. She toasts the man in the audience but never stops singing. The waiter removes the bottles.

"What happens to the booze?" I ask

"It gets thrown away," Alison tells me.

"Why?" I am amazed.

"Shows how wealthy he is," Alison replies. The songs are long and plaintive and the rhythm is eastern. I see now how different we are as I watch the people around me. I don't understand the codes here, can't tell who is who. The wealthiest dress like peasants, peasants dress like bank clerks, the powerful lurk in dark corners. In the village I was disconnected. Here in the town I am part of something. I am living. The customers in the restaurant tell me how lucky I am, to be part of real island life. But I know that I am not part of it. So tonight I am out with local boys, tomorrow I will sit in a bar with the ex-pats. Perhaps I am safer with them. I belong to neither group but I'll spend a while marking time like this until I decide what to do and where to go next.

According to Doug's directions I should walk around the harbour to the far side, past the café where I'd first met him and his wife, Alison.

'Keep to the sea front, don't go down the passage on your right.' He had been quite insistent. The passage seemed harmless enough, as I peered down I could see doorways to sorry-looking bars, the cobbles were dark black and the air smelled a bit damp. Walking as instructed, past an ancient building with a crumbling dome, used as a museum or gallery which housed an exhibition on sea turtles, I carried on to the marina. Small vessels bobbed on the lapping waves and I stopped to listen to the ping, ping as a rope tapped against the mast of a yacht, and buoys banged dully between boats and the harbour wall. I loved these sounds and the slap, slap as the water hit the ancient stones.

Just as Doug had described, to the right was a paved square, where cars were parked nose-to-nose. Behind these was a long low building which had a wooden pergola running its length. Under this were tables set for the evening trade. In front of the restaurant stood an old ship's wheel with a carved wooden sign leaned against it showing the name of the taverna. I recognised Doug and Alison taking their seats at one of the outside tables. A waiter came over to speak to them.

I walked purposefully up to their table, pulling my scarf around me, like a comforter. The waiter ceased talking, abruptly, then muttered something to Doug, bowed his head slightly and disappeared through the doorway into the kitchen. Doug looked across at Alison and stood up to greet me.

"You came!" A broad smile stretched across his face. Alison smiled gently and patted the chair next to hers.

"You look so like your mother."

"You knew her well?" As soon as she spoke Alison's face tensed.

"Very well," she whispered. "Doug and I helped her leave, take you back to England."

"Was she so unhappy?" I wanted desperately to believe that life had been good. "Surely my father looked out for us?" Alison's brow pulled down and she laughed, a sharp sound in her throat.

"Oh yeah, your father certainly kept a watchful eye!" The change in Alison shocked me, but I pushed on.

"I know my mother could be difficult..." Alison cut me off mid sentence.

"Difficult? Anna was a sweet, lively girl. She had time and energy for everyone she met. She could be wild and unpredictable, but she was alive and fresh." Doug rested his hand on his wife's.

"Shh. Keep calm, people will hear."

"And what if they do? They all knew him, they all knew what he was like – king of the bloody castle."

"Tell me then," I pleaded. "Tell me what he was like, she told me nothing at all, just stories."

"Your father had his eye on her from the minute she arrived in town."

"Before that," said Doug

"Am I telling this?" Alison flashed at him.

"I'll get some drinks, order food." Doug disappeared inside the taverna, leaving me with Alison at the table. She stroked my face. It was strange, I'm not really a hugging, stroking kind of person, but with these two, it seemed kind of natural. I didn't feel that usual freeze.

"You are so like her, around the eyes, the way you sit even." She held my hand.

"She said she met him in the village, where she worked when she first came here. She was beautiful."

"She still is." I insisted, frightened to use the past tense. I knew my mother was alive, but it seemed that for Doug and Alison she had ceased to exist.

"Sometimes I look at her and wonder how she can be my mother." Alison smiled and continued.

"When she came into my restaurant that day, she was flushed and nervous, he had been following her. He never liked me, kept away. I've met his sort before."

"What sort?"

"The controlling sort. Such a creep! A controlling bastard! He made sure she needed him, he stripped her of her friends, he kept her close, watched her. She had no friends out there in the village, and when she met Karen he tried to put a stop to that too. But he didn't scare Karen either." Alison seemed like a different person as she spoke, her eyes narrowed, her face hardened. She seemed angry and that frightened me.

"We'd never seen him before, us Brits, but the locals knew him. The old women used to whisper about him, the men loathed him but never stood up to him. Nobody knew where he was from. He's not from here you know? 'Up North' they used to say. The old ones used to tell ghost stories about him, how he'd lived here for centuries, put the willies up us all. They told us to let him have your mum. They said she'd never want for anything, 'he has olives, land', but they wouldn't want him after their daughter. Mind you he wasn't interested in the local girls, it was tourist girls he watched. Don't get me wrong, he wasn't a kamaki."

"Kamaki?"

"It means spear," Doug had come back with a pitcher of wine and some glasses. "They call those guys kamaki, or say they would make kamaki, those guys who chase women. A hunter, a player, you know." Alison glared at him for interrupting and continued her story.

"Anyway, that's not what your dad was. He was picky. It was Anna he wanted. It seemed like anytime there was any trouble he was there to sort it out. He gave me the creeps, watching her like a hawk all the time. If she so much as looked at another guy he turned black with rage! He would fluff himself up and go crazy! That time she went to the harbour with you," she gestured to Doug.
He nodded, "he would change, into something else."

"For Christ's sake Doug! Let it go will you." Alison spun to look at Doug at the end of the table. "The guy was a bully, plain and simple. An overbearing, insensitive prick! Classic low-self-esteem-bullying-prick!"

"He picked her flowers, she told me. He loved her." My chest felt tight and the words caught halfway up my throat. I needed to hear some good about the man who was my father.

"Oh yes he loved her, he used to beg her to stay, cry in her lap, she told me that. Not as much as she used to cry to me!" Alison's head dropped. Doug stretched his hand out to her and tried to reach her fingers.

"I'm sorry." She was crying now. I felt panicked. Nothing they said made sense.

"Can you just tell me what happened, why we left?"
Doug spoke.

"Your mother was afraid. She saw less and less of her friends. He made it difficult. When we visited, it was awkward, he made us feel awkward. We used to try and go when we thought he wouldn't be around, but Anna wouldn't relax. She worried what he would say when he came back. Then there was the thing with the birds."

"For heaven's sake! There was nothing with the birds," Alison interrupted this time.

"Anna said,"

"Anna said! Anna said! You know the state she was in!"

"Please, both of you. Please tell me one story." Doug held up his hand to her and nodded towards the waiter who was approaching with their food. They waited quietly while he set down the dishes and plates and a boy followed with a basket of bread. The waiter looked across at me and said something to Doug, who nodded in reply.

"What did he say?" I asked.

"That you're like your mother," replied Alison.

"That we should be careful," said Doug.

"There you go again Doug. What is it with you? Can't you be pleased she's here?"

"Of course, I'm pleased to see her." I picked up my glass and drank some wine. It tasted familiar, and warming.

"Look," I hesitated. "Something happened at home. I'd gone away and she was alone. When I called her she said she was coming back to sort it out with him. She had these ideas, the stories. Sometimes I think she believed them. But she's missing and I think she may be here. I know that she loved this island, but I know that she was afraid of coming here. I know that she loved the sea but would never go near it. I know she was depressed, but I don't know why."

"Ally," Doug began.

"No, wait." Alison interrupted. "Let me." She stroked Doug's hand and smiled before beginning her story again.

"Ally, your mother would never come back here. She met your father quite soon after she came to the island. He wooed her I suppose. It seemed quite romantic in a creepy kind of way. There was no doubt he wanted to be with her, everyone said so. He was always there when she needed him, like magic. One night on the way home she stumbled on some men attacking Doug and she tried to stop them," she reached forward for Doug's hand as she spoke. "Your father turned up and got rid of them. Then another time we'd been out for the day, a whole group of us and there was an accident. One of the boys was badly hurt and while we were all wondering what to do he turned up out of nowhere and dealt with it all, the hospital, doctors, police, everything. No awkward questions, no blame. Anna went to the hospital with the injured boy."

"He was dead," whispered Doug. Alison shot him a glance before continuing.

"After that he took her away to stay at his house in the mountains. We didn't know where she was, just that she was with him. After a week or so we saw them in the harbour, like a couple, always arm in arm or hand in hand. She seemed happy."

"Then she told us she was going to have a baby with him," Doug interrupted again, "just like that."

"Not I'm pregnant but I'm going to try for a baby," Alison went on, glaring at him to keep quiet. "Then when she got pregnant, she came to me, upset. He went crazy for a while, like he didn't want a child, when it had been his idea all along. But then he was okay and she was happy, but she was lonely." Doug butted in again.

"Sometimes he'd leave her in that house with no transport or money."

"She had you, they called you their princess and it seemed like life was good. But it was in the winter he used to change."

"She was alone too much," Doug again.

Alison nodded her agreement.

"She needed company and he kept her from it. Then there were his moods. She said he would change. He frightened her. He told her wild stories about himself, he would threaten her. At first she used to laugh at him, try and bring him out of the moods, but over time he wore her down until she wasn't the same sparky girl anymore," Alison hung her head and looked away.

"So we helped her get out, " finished Doug.

"Did he know we were leaving?"

"No. You left one morning."

"On a motorbike." I closed my eyes and smelled earth and warmth, hot close bodies, sound of an engine. "I remember something. She never told me."

"We didn't take you. Andy drove you on his bike. A mad old drunk who worked on the farm next to your house. He wasn't afraid of Korakas."

"Korakas?"

"That's what they called your dad. It means crow."

"She's afraid of crows," I said, "but she paints them too."

"Afraid, how?" Doug leant forward and stared hard at Ally.

"Oh Doug," Alison rolled her eyes. Doug raised a hand as if to quiet her.

"Afraid how?" He repeated.

"Just that she used to shout at them, when she had an episode." Doug looked blankly at her so she carried on. "She had episodes, of depression I suppose. Something would trigger it and then she would rant and scream, or lock herself away, withdraw. She took tablets once, but I asked her not to. They didn't really help. She seemed unhappy, that's all and we all get unhappy sometimes."

"What about the crows?"

"There are these trees at home."

"Poplars, in the lane," Alison spoke now.

"I don't know what they are."

"They're poplars," said Doug.

"It's Doug's house. He bought it years ago when he was based in the UK."

"Your house? I don't understand."

"She had nowhere to take you. She had to get out, so we sorted it out for her." I stood up and took a step away from the table. My head ached. I pulled my scarf close to me again, for comfort and breathed in to inhale its smell, but there was nothing.

"That's my home."

Doug spoke quickly,

"yes it is and it always will be. I swear!" It wasn't the first house we lived in, we moved around a lot, but it was the only one I remembered. When mum opened the door on the day we moved in, we were greeted by a heavy scent. A bowl full of yellow flowers stood on the table in the hall. We walked through and into the kitchen, there too, every surface held a bowl or a jar or a vase of them. The whole house was full of them. As we climbed the stairs each step had some and the bathroom and the bedrooms. I thought I might have dreamed it or heard it in a story, but mum told me it was true. She said I used to ask her if we would stay at the yellow house.

"The day we moved in it was full of flowers, every room. Yellow."

"That was my idea, to make her feel welcome," said Alison. "Daffodils. Anna loved yellow. I wanted it to be spring for her, a new beginning. She had such a bad few months when she first took you back. She couldn't go to the house straight away, we had to move the tenants out first and make sure he didn't know where it was." Alison stood up and joined Doug at my side as I stood there, not sure what to do, but I pulled away.

"I have to go. I don't understand any of this. Nothing makes sense. She told me nothing but stories and now you tell me new ones."

"Alithea," Alison was coaxing now. "Baby. We tried to protect you and I've told you now. Your father was controlling, a bully, damaged I suppose. She made a mistake, but she had you. That's what matters. She had a beautiful baby girl and look at you now, you're a woman."

"Please. I need to find my mother. I don't have anybody else, she doesn't have anybody else. I think she's come here." Alison frowned,

"Alithea, did you contact the police at all? If you're worried about her..."

I shook my head, "I'm sure this is where she is."

"I don't think she would ever come back here," said Doug, "but I'll help you as much as I can. Anna's our family, so are you. Maybe I can show you around, help you understand this place. Would that help?"

I nodded, but these people made me more afraid for what might have happened to my mum.

"No fairy tales, Doug," said Alison. Doug laughed.

"No fairy tales!"

Nikos is in his usual seat outside the restaurant, reading the paper while keeping half an eye on the passers-by. He owns one of the bars on the front. His daughter is with him today. I wonder if she knows he's had a girl friend here in town for the past three years? I've never met his wife. She stays up on Akrotiri, the peninsula to the east, where they have a huge villa with a sea view. Perhaps she's happier that way, she has her life and he has his. Jan, one of the girls who works 'outside' his bar turns up. They call working behind the bar 'inside', those girls earn more money. If you work 'outside' it's your job to sit at the bar and drink with the customers, encouraging them to spend more. They dance a bit. Some of them I know, do more than that if they fancy it, a freelance kind of thing, for drinks and dinner and treats. I don't know how old Jan is, could be forty, might be thirty. The drink has taken its toll as the season has progressed and she looks wrecked today. Nikos calls me over.

"Anna, bring a beer for Jan will you?" I can see she's been crying. Nikos sends his daughter off with some money, on some errand and once she has gone he leans across to Jan and wipes her face gently. I hear him say,

"Tell no-one. I will deal with this." His daughter is back and he calls me over again.

"Anna, take Jan home will you, get her some food from here." He throws down more money, but Alison, who has been watching with me, shakes her head.

"We'll sort her out. Leave it to me".

"I don't want him involved." He seems agitated and jerks his head towards the street. I look up and see that man again. He is walking across the street towards us.

"Nikos?" Their voices are raised but I don't understand what they're saying. Nikos is angry but seems afraid. He lowers his head,

63

like the boy who was scolded across the street that time before.

"What are they saying?" I ask Alison.

"I can't hear it all. But Jan got into trouble at the bar last night. Nikos' cousin and some of his friends stayed on late with her. It got.." she sighed,

"...out of hand. She should go to the police, but they won't take much notice of a bar girl. That's what's made Korakas go crazy".

"Korakas?"

"That's what they call your friend – The Crow."

The man leans towards Nikos and spits out, "Keep control of your family!"

Nikos says something quietly and I thought I saw Korakas raise his hand to him, but he lowered it again quickly.

"Control them or I will!" Then he's gone. Jan is white-faced, Nikos is pacing, smoking and swearing. His daughter is quiet, unsure what to do next. I take Jan by the arm and start to walk her on up the street, to get her away from it all. The streets are narrow here. Each restaurant has tables and chairs outside and the shops display their goods. The owners and workers watch as we pass, all of them must have heard what's gone on. I put my arm around Jan's waist and ask her which street she lives on. She points up the hill. It is like a labyrinth back here. The harbour was built by the Venetians, the houses rise high on either side and seem to lean in towards each other, obscuring the sky. I can smell the earthy musk of trailing geraniums which are planted in old olive oil cans painted in bright colours. Cats line our way, sleeping, sitting, washing, watching. Jan leads me, leaning into me and I keep hold of her waist. We reach a house at the end of an alleyway and Jan fumbles in her bag, producing a key. As she pulls it out a photograph falls. I pick it up and hand it back to her. Two children, smiling, wearing school uniform She snatches it and holds it to her.

"My kids. They live with their dad." We hadn't spoken until then.

"Should I come in?" I ask her.

"It was my own fault," is all she says, and slips through the door, closing it quickly behind her, leaving me alone. I hesitate. I am unsure which way we turned into this street. I am cold again. One of the cats yowls as if it has been kicked, and there he is at the corner. Korakas.

"I hate cats," he says. He frightens me, but I don't know why. I take a guess at which way we came and head off, brushing past him as I turn back towards the harbour. He touches my arm, in that way he has. I stop and look up at him. My face is burning hot. He seems taller and broader here in the dark street. His hair glistens so dark the black is almost green. His voice is rasping.

"Don't get mixed up with these types."

"These types?" I am incredulous.

"You are a clean girl."

"You sound like a village woman." He tightens his grip on my arm.

"Do not involve yourself. I can deal with all of this, it is not for you."

"Don't tell me what to do!" I pull my arm away and run past, tripping on the cobbles. He reaches out and steadies me. His voice changes when he speaks, now he is gentle. I feel like a child.

"Anna, I protect my people and I will protect you." His voice is calm as he holds me still, but he is not at rest. His eyes take in the street and the sky and the roof-tops. I pull against him and look away. I can see a woman walking up the alley from the harbour. Undoubtedly English. She is wearing a strapless dress and her shoulders are burned as pink as the bougainvillea she is admiring. Her hat is one of the harbour trader's finest and she is carrying one of the handmade leather bags which will never lose its dead cow smell. The sight of her gives me the strength to break away from him and I walk, run, towards her. She looks at me as I pass by and I turn to see if he is following, but he has already gone.

I woke up early and set out to find some breakfast at the café on the corner. A truck blocked the passageway which lead to the harbour front and I had to squeeze past it to get by. The driver nodded and smiled at me, before opening the door and swinging up behind the steering wheel.

"An early start," I looked across in the direction the voice had come from to see that man again – the one who had been outside my room when I first arrived, the one who had picked up my scarf. I smiled involuntarily, perhaps because I'd been smiling at the driver already. He stepped towards me and fell into step beside me as I walked on down to the harbourfront. I felt flushed, embarrassed, conscious of every movement I made. Annoyed at a desire to appear appealing to him, even though he irritated me.

"Will you take coffee with me?" He held his hands up as if I was holding a gun at him. Laughing he tilted his head in a mock bow, "I am not kamaki!" That word again.

"I'm meeting a friend." I felt foolish, as if I was making excuses. He made me feel like a child, awkward and inexperienced. His fingers brushed my elbow as we walked, almost touching, almost steering. As we reached the café on the corner, where I'd seen Doug and Alison on that first day, I hesitated. He took me by the arm and led me towards a table.

"Don't be afraid," he leant towards me as he pulled out the chair for me to sit.

"I'm not afraid!"

"Alithea?" I was shocked at the use of my name, and then I was afraid and frowned.

"How do you know my name?"

"My apologies, it is a word meaning 'truth' or 'truly'. You

66

seemed a little afraid of me."

"Oh! That's my name." What a fool to tell a complete stranger my name.

"It is a good name." He beckoned to the waiter and ordered coffees and we sat in silence until they arrived. I looked out to sea and let my mind drift. For the first time since I'd arrived I felt relaxed. The air was clear, sounds came and went around me, voices, mopeds, a dog barking, a woman calling after a child. The smell of coffee interrupted my thoughts and I felt my mother close, as if she were sitting right next to me. I stretched out my fingers on the table and jumped as I realised I'd touched his hand. The coffees had arrived and as I looked back from the sea to the table, he was watching me.

"I'm sorry, you must think me very strange." I pulled my hand away. "I'm not on holiday you see, I'm meeting somebody. I'm looking for somebody." His eyes narrowed, his features seemed to sharpen as his eyebrows pulled forward.

"There are many people here who do not wish to be found." As he spoke I heard my name called in the distance and swung my head around to see who it was. Doug was walking, half running towards us, waving and calling. He looked faintly ridiculous and I felt embarrassed for him. I turned back to look at the man, he had thrown some money on the table and stood to leave. He called out to the waiter and waved at the table as he disappeared around the corner into the alleyway which ran behind the café. Doug, out of breath, sat down at the table.

"Who's the old guy?" He pushed the empty coffee cup roughly away.

"Old guy?" I was confused, I'd put him a few years older than me, five, maybe. Perhaps more. His skin was fresh and smooth like a younger man's, but his eyes were dark and deep, as if they had seen a lifetime of visions. He had the confidence of an older man, a sense of ease about him.

"The guy? Who is he?" Doug's voice strained.

"I don't know. I've seen him around. He just bought me coffee, that's all."

"I don't like you speaking to strangers!"

"Doug," I said softly, touched by his concern, "you're a stranger too, remember?"

"I suppose I am." He lifted his head to look straight at me and stretched out his hand to hold mine, "but you must remember that I held you when you were tiny, I watched you learn to walk, heard your first words. You and Anna are family to me and to Alison. Your mother named you for her."

"I hadn't realised, of course!"

"Your dad gave her no choice in the matter, he'd chosen your name, said you needed a strong name to live up to. She laughed when she told us because he'd been so insistent about it and hadn't realised that she'd call you Ally, after Alison. Man, he loathed Alison back then!"

"She doesn't seem too keen on him either."

"He did everything he could to keep Anna away from her friends and yet he would leave her for days when you were born."

"Did he ever hurt her?"

"Not like you mean. He did control her, manipulate her. He is very strong."

"Go on."

"I believe there are different explanations. My wife's a straight talker, she's direct. It's black or white, cut 'n' dried. Me? I've seen stuff, met people. I believe stuff. Your dad, he's not from round here. Nobody knows where he's from. He used to tell your mom stories, people used to tell us stories."

"Fairy-stories?"

"Kind of. That night I got beat up? Like Al said. One night I was walking back to the hotel from the harbour, this guy called out to me. I knew what he was up to, we got told, 'watch yourself,' some of these guys hate the US boys. I stopped because he called me, then walked on, but another one jumped me and dragged me down an alley, just up from where you're staying. I can show you. Come on. Let's start the tour."

He put his hand out to me to show me the way and together we retraced the steps back around the harbourfront to my hotel.

"Just a little further," Doug smiled at me and walked slightly ahead, then stopped. "Here." He stopped at the entrance to an alley, which ran up to a high wall, a dead end. Together we walked in, the air was damp. I breathed in the scent of my scarf, blocking the smell of decay and damp, as we continued.

"It was here, right at the end. Thought I was done for, when I heard your mom, screaming at them to stop. I tried to send her away. I knew they'd do her as well. They don't care, tourists, incomers, we ask for what we get, they say. Then he came, your dad, like some great wind hurtling down past her and he knocked them to hell, sent them begging, on their knees. He caught one of them across the side of the face, like he'd been hit by a truck. Held your mom against him while he sent them flying. Like no man I've ever seen. He was tall, scared the shit out of me and he was on my side. Where did he come from? Three men he took on, but they didn't fight, they just cowered and begged to be let go. There was that sound, like a wind - blood rushing in my ears Al said - I was pretty beat up - in shock the M.O. at the base said. He was there and then he was gone. He did that, came from nowhere, then gone again."

I touched Doug's arm.

"But Doug, this is my father we're talking about."

"Al's right, no fairy-stories. He used to scare your mom with stories, they're what pushed her over the edge. Then I'd hear stuff from other people. Maybe it is all in my head. It's just that so much doesn't add up. Why didn't he follow you to England? He loved you both like a mad man, he went wild when you'd gone."

"So why didn't he?"

"Vrykolakas can't cross the sea." I watched Doug as he spoke, the muscles in his neck twitched and his eyes flicked from one side of the alley to the other. I laid my hand on his arm and he flinched.

"I don't understand. Tell me what kind of man he was."

"I didn't know him like that. He kept apart."

"Then tell me the stories."

"I'll show you where he kept your mother and you until she took you away. But don't tell Al. She'd take a swipe at me if she knew.

69

It's late in the season. I sit in the kafeneon on the corner and watch as the few late tourists walk by. We talk and exchange gossip. A favourite sport is to fill in clues in Alison's crossword when she's not looking. I call out, "entanglement!"

"What?" She is irritated.

"Seven down, entanglement."

"Thanks." She says, meaning quite the opposite. There are a lot of Americans around now, posted over here. Navy flyers on tour of duty before heading back home. They mean well, good tippers, but not really welcome. Some bars won't have them in. They don't understand why they should be banned. They don't understand much it seems. Alison has one after her. She protests.

"A short American! Is that the best I can do?" But we know she likes him.

"What you been up to today?" She asks as one of them orders a beer.

"Just chasin' clouds," he answers in deep southern drawl. Sometimes they do a low fly past the harbour to show off. He flashes us a smile. We cringe, but smile back. They are so American and we are so English. I look around the tables. An ex publican, the biker couple, classics graduate, bouncer, waitress, teacher, mechanic, chef, retired MD. The American table, navy flyers, officers and ranks, the Syrians, German Kris, Swedish Lou, the Danish sisters, Nikos and his bar girls. Where else would we sit together, talk together? I watch the classics grad climb onto her motorbike and kick it into life, the mechanic jumps on behind her, wrapping his arms round her waist, they drive off.

As soon as Alison has finished her crossword we head off for the old Turkish baths – they serve great food there. The baths lie empty and are filled with tables and chairs now. Some Serbian guy is playing a guitar. The part where we like to sit is open to the sky. It feels good to be at a table eating, surrounded by high stone walls and the canopy of the night sky. Conversation is easy. It rolls in circles, we have heard many of the stories before, but that's comforting. Stories about the island, not the lives we lived before. We make our own history together.

I am tired and decide to leave before the others and walk once round the harbour front before I head off home. The alley runs parallel to the harbour and I walk confidently in the dark towards the turning down to the sea. I hear a noise and look to my left. A group of men is huddled at the end of the narrow opening between houses. I stop. That noise again. I focus my eyes, I can see that they are holding someone. I walk towards them and I hear a voice,

"No, Anna, go!" It is Alison's short American. I am angry. He is a placid man, a gentle person. His voice is muffled. One of the men breaks away from the group and walks towards me. I know I have made a mistake. I know I should run now, but I stay because I know that if I run the American will be badly hurt. My mind races over the stories I have heard, like Jan and those men at Nikos' bar. There was a man who had been beaten on his way back to his hotel, took a wrong turn, ended up in jail because he fought back. I stepped forward.

"Let him go." They begin to whistle at me, calling to me. I don't understand the words but I get the message. Now two of them are moving towards me, but I keep walking and shouting at them, anything to let them know I'm not afraid and to let the American know that I won't leave him alone. But I am afraid, wishing I had walked on, but knowing that if I had I would never be able to look Al in the face again.

I raise my arms and scream at them. "Fige! Fige!" Like Chrissoula used to scream at the cats to go away. They stop and I laugh, because fear has made me hysterical. They stand, one still holding the American against the wall, but all looking towards me, past me. A rush of wind comes up the alley and almost pushes me over, the noise is like the sea crashing onto rocks. I steady myself against the damp wall and turn to see Korakas. He stands tall, blocking the feeble light from the houses on the street. He has his arms raised, as I had done and he is screeching at them. His eyes are alight, his hair is flying in the strange wind and his features seem angular. Suddenly he is beside me and holds me close to him, snatching me away from the two men in front of me. He sweeps his other arm in front of his face and sends one of the men sprawling to the floor, where he lies limp, blood trickling from a cut on his head. The other man drops to his knees and crawls towards his friend, sobbing and begging. The others are crossing themselves and half run half crawl to aid their friends at our feet. Korakas sweeps his coat across in front of my face and moves towards the American. The men scrabble to get out of his way. He holds me around my waist and stoops to help the American. I can feel my legs weaken and I am glad of his support. He walks with us, back towards the harbour where normal night-life is playing out. He sits me at a table in a small bar and sets the American opposite.

"Wait here." The first words he has spoken.

Before long two Americans arrive and help Al's short friend home.

"Thank you," I say.

"I did this for you, not them." He looks very ordinary across the table, dark hair, dark eyes, average build. He pushes a small shot glass of clear spirit across the table towards me. It is tsikouthia, distilled from grapes. I drink it down. As it warms my throat and chest it brings back a childhood memory, sneaked handfuls of currants from the carefully weighed out ingredients for the Christmas cake. I am homesick again. A sound begins in my chest and I cannot form it into a word. He puts his hand over mine and strokes it.

Doug walked me to the square where he'd parked his car and we didn't speak as he navigated his way through the streets and out of town. I leaned out of the window and breathed in the smells. He drove carefully as the road wove its way further up the side of the mountain. It was warm and he wore a short-sleeved shirt, one arm hanging out of the open window on his side of the car.

"Your dad had a house up here. When he first met your mom, he brought her up. We didn't see her for a while. It's hard to find." As he spoke he was scanning the landscape. The road bent to the left, dangerously close to the edge of the hillside, they passed a sign for a taverna, boasting the best view on the island.

"Not far now." Doug accelerated and rounded another corner before pulling off the road between two olive trees. The car bounced along a track.

"This doesn't look right." He stopped the car. "It's been a while since I came up here. Not since she took you away to be honest."

"Maybe you took a wrong turn."

"This is how it goes."

"What goes?" I was laughing, until I turned to look at Doug.

"It was here. It still is. Get out the car." I did as I was told, and followed Doug as he wove his way between the trees, along a path, which might have been wide enough for a car at some time.

"It's like an enchanted forest!" I laughed again. In front of us was a crumbling wall, the remains of what must have been a dwelling at some time. Beneath our feet the path was cobbled, rough grass growing up between the stones.

"This can't be it." I shook my head as I looked around.

"Come on." Doug held out his hand to me but I walked

past him and followed the line of the wall around. I stepped over the stones and walked down a tree-lined track which led to a fence. Beyond this I could see poly-tunnels, empty, as far as I could tell from where I was standing. Doug stood quietly beside me.

"This can't be it," he said. He turned and walked back the way they had come. "She made a home out here. We visited, not very often, but it was always a home. In the winter, she was afraid, sometimes he would leave her alone, with you, while he went off for days. I think he did it to make her afraid, to keep her in check. She said he left the birds to watch her."

"You make him sound so cruel."

"He… she was afraid of him, but they did love each other." Doug's hands were shaking. I took hold of one and began to walk back to the car, leading him behind me. I glanced back at him,

"I'm so afraid of what's happened to mum. I need to find her."

"We'll ask around, see what we can do. If she's come here we'll find her," he said reassuringly, "after all, it's only been a couple of days. Does she know how to contact you?"

"I lost my mobile." Silently cursing Rachel, I ran back to the car and waited for Doug to catch up.

"Slow down, I'm an old guy remember?"

Alison and the short American have finally got it together. He is laughing about his near death experience and how it made Al realise how much he meant to her. He doesn't seem bothered that a gang of local men wanted him dead for no apparent reason.

"Everyone hates Americans here!" He laughs. His lip is swollen and he has a cut over one eye. He's told me what a fool I was to try and help, but he keeps buying me drinks.

"Don't know what'd have happened if your friend hadn't showed up."

"He's not my friend." I sound like a petulant child.
Nikos is glowering over his paper in the corner.

"Dangerous friend to have."

"My kind of friend if you ask me" laughs Al. "What's your problem with him?"

"Xeni." He mutters to himself.

"Foreigners? Is that us? Or him as well?" He doesn't reply.

"Is that the problem Nikos? He's a foreigner who's stuck his nose in and tried to sort you lot out!"

Al is slapping a damp cloth across the tables, like she's slapping Nikos' face and her voice is shaking.

"First Jan and now Doug?" So it's Doug now, not Shorty.

"You and your village mob get handy and some foreigner comes in and gets the better of you."

"Shut your mouth, woman! You know nothing about that man. Where's he from? What does he do? What does he want with Anna?"

"So where is he from?" I ask, very quietly. I don't want to be associated with that man. I have an easy life here. The conflict begins whenever he is near. Maybe I should move on. Maybe I have already stayed too long. It felt good to be part of a community again.

But when I'm alone I can be invisible, now I feel exposed.

"He's from the North," mutters Nikos.

"Ela morai, tell them who he really is." Nikos' cousin, his arm heavily bandaged, has joined him at his table. Al looks up when she hears his voice.

"I don't want you in here."

"Wait," says Doug, "let him tell us. Is he the bogey man?" Nikos throws some money on the table and gets up to leave.

"Ela, come," he nods to his cousin. "Pame, let's go."

"Who is he?" I shout as they walk away. The other traders in the street watch as they walk past and look back towards me. Some shake their heads and turn back to their work. The yiayia across the street grins at me, baring the few teeth she has left and chuckles as she rocks on her chair. The atmosphere is sour. Al isn't talking. Doug is morose, nursing his aching ribs. Only a couple of customers have appeared for the evening session. I make some excuse and leave. As I walk past her shop, the old yiayia hisses at me, "vrykolakas," and cackles.

I was so frustrated. The days were slipping by and I'd achieved nothing. This town had that effect on me. A kind of sleep had come over me. What used to seem so pressing just wasn't anymore. Even my usual pace of walking had slowed to a nonchalant stroll. I kept seeing that man, the one who had bought me coffee. It didn't seem strange though, as there were so many familiar faces in the harbour. People seemed to sit drinking coffee. More tourists walked the streets now, as the season shifted into full swing, yet I was aware of how quiet it was as I walked back to my room each night. I was finding it hard to remember how many days I'd been here already. Today I was going to try and hook up with Doug and Alison again. I had no address for them, or telephone number. To meet here it seemed you just hung around where you expected a person to be. With this in mind I set out for the kafeneon on the corner.

The waiter smiled broadly at me, making me feel instantly at ease. He beckoned to me to sit nearer the back of the tables outside. I had noticed that most of the tourists sat at the front, but the locals made their way closer to the door of the café and watched the comings and goings of all the clientele. He held a chair for me to sit and then as quickly as his smile had arrived, it went again. His eyes flicked away from me and as I followed their direction, I saw that man, walking towards us. The waiter muttered something and backed off. The man approached, oblivious to the waiter, and held out his hand to me.

"Alithea. Kalimera. We meet again." He closed both his hands around mine and nodded his head slightly. "So, will you take coffee with me again?"

He was so self-assured. I felt myself bristle slightly. I felt flattered at the attention and yet irritated at my reaction to him.

"I really am meeting somebody."

"This you tell me, every time we meet. You are looking for somebody. I remember. Tell me who is it that you seek?" As I was about to answer, I heard a shriek.

"Oh My God!" A woman's voice. "It is you. It's you!" My companion reacted as if scalded, pushing the chair back quickly and rushing inside. He usually seemed so calm and relaxed, but as soon as I turned to see where he had gone a woman leapt into the seat he had just left and squealed with delight.

"What an idiot! I thought you were Anna for a moment, and sitting next to him too! You're the baby aren't you? Anna's baby? My baby princess! I never believed for a minute I'd see you again! Oh come here!" She lunged at me and grabbed me in her arms, squeezing the breath out of me. She had spoken so rapidly, firing the words into the air and now she sat deflated. Her round face shone and a couple of tears popped into her eyes.

"And where the hell has he gone?" She looked around and I realised she meant the stranger.

"I have no idea, he seemed to run off when he heard your voice."

"Damn right he would as well. Baby Ally, where's your mum?"

"I'm sorry. I have no idea who you are. I am Ally, Anna's daughter, but.."

"I'm Karen. I was your mum's neighbour when you were tiny. We used to bake together you and I. So where is she and what are you doing back here?"

I felt sick. Each time I explained about my mother I felt less certain that I would be able to find her. And as I explained, Karen's face dissolved in front of me.

"What do you mean you don't know where she is?" Her soft face became rigid. She began picking at the skin around her nails as she spoke, her eyes flitting about as if she would see Anna at any moment.

"She has been well though hasn't she? I mean, her mind? You know she was," she hesitated, "unsettled, here?"

"I grew up with my mother's depression. I didn't know that's what it was as a child, I just thought she got upset about stuff. But she did fun stuff as well."

Some nights, when I was small, I would hear mum crying. I would creep down the stairs into the kitchen and find her sitting in her favourite chair at the table. I would climb up into her lap and pat her shoulder, just like she used to pat mine when I was unhappy. We rocked gently to and fro and I would say "Shh. Shh," like mum did to me. I didn't know why she cried, but it was mainly at night. During the day we laughed a lot and played games. When I was older she admitted to me that she was afraid of the dark and yet she had always seemed so brave. We never locked the doors, except last thing at night. We never drew the curtains because she liked to look out at the sky.

Never show your fear Ally, she told me. If you are afraid, hold your head high and keep going. Face the things that frighten you most head on.

Karen sighed.

"She was always fun, except towards the end and then she became more and more paranoid. The trouble is there's so many stories in a place like this, it's hard to know what to believe and what not to."

"My mother raised me on fairy stories." I'd said the line countless times, to countless people. Whenever I was questioned about my birth place, or my father, I would resort to that. "My mother raised me on fairy stories." An attempt to divert attention from the fact I knew very little at all. Karen took my hand and began to speak quietly, closing her eyes.

"Do you remember? 'Once upon a time there was a beautiful princess, the most special child in a magical kingdom, where food was plenty and the sun shone. Her skin was as white as the snow on the tops of the mountains, her eyes like dark roasted almonds, her hair as golden as the sand on the beaches. The Dark King had stolen the land. In the summer the people were warm and happy and wanted for nothing, but in the winter he would bring down terrible storms to show his might and keep his people from disobeying him. The king was unhappy because he was trapped on the island by a terrible curse. He knew how much the people loved the princess and he knew that if he held her captive the people would obey him for fear he would harm her. But the people helped the princess escape to protect her, even though they were left to suffer at his hands."

I sighed.

"My mother used to tell me those stories. Is that why we ran away? Because an unhappy king wanted to keep us captive? Really?" Karen, pulled her hand away and laughed.

"It's just a story darling, just a story."

"That's what she used to say too."

"What else did she say?" Karen leant forward and looked closely at me.

"That birds don't make good fathers."

"Now you're making fun and it's not funny." Karen was angry.

"I'm sorry. I don't mean to upset you and I don't think any of this is funny. I'm in the dark here. None of you tell it how it is and all I want to know is if you can help me find my mother. Who would she contact if she came back here?"

"Listen to me. I don't think your mother would ever come back here."

"So why did you call out like that when you saw me? As if you expected her?"

"Because I've been thinking about her, thought I saw her a few days ago. I miss her even now." I grabbed at Karen's hand,

"Where? Where did you see her?"

"It doesn't matter. I'm always seeing things! Just ask anyone, they think I'm barking mad. But I felt Anna was close, now I know it must have been you. You were here and that's what I could feel."

"But she said she was coming here. Doug says that my father…"

"You've spoken to Doug and Alison?"

"I met them soon after I arrived, by chance, like I've met

80

you now."

"I don't see them so much now. I don't come down much anymore."

"Down?"

"I live on the peninsula now. I moved soon after you and your mum left. It was hard when you'd gone. Your father went crazy for a while. I didn't want to be so close once you'd left."

"Did he try and come after us?"

"He couldn't do that."

"Oh yeah, he can't cross water! That's right." I was tired of all this.

"His life is here."

"I thought my mother was his life?"

"And she was, so were you. He laid low once you'd gone. Not much sign of him at all, until today I thought that was him."

"Today?"

"With you."

"He's just some man, besides he's too young."

"Korakas never looked his age." I had a sudden thought,

"If I could find him, I might be able to find her." Karen grabbed my hand again, "don't go looking for him, he may be your father by blood, but you know nothing about him. Your mother did right taking you away." I pulled my hand back and stood up quickly.

"None of you seem to want to help! Alison said my father was a bully, Doug thinks he's some kind of spook."

"Shh! Don't shout." Karen glanced around to see who was watching.

"Telling me what to do all the time. I'm not a little kid and I know something is going on here. I'm sick of the secrets. If none of you will help me I'll find someone who can." I ran through the tables and down towards the harbour front, leaving Karen at the table.

As I rounded the corner, I heard my name called, "Alithea!" Sat astride a motorbike was the stranger again. I was angry with Karen and upset. Seeing him, I remembered a time I'd been lost at a market as a small child. I'd lost sight of mum, for just a moment, but when I found her again, I felt angry at her, abandoned. I snapped at him.

"Where did you go?"

"I go where I please!" His face contorted, seemed sharper, but then he laughed. "Women like that! I can't stand them. Stupid harbour witches. I don't stick around when they're close by."

"She was a friend of my mother's."

"Strange company she kept," he said dismissively. Then offering his hand, "Ela, come, take a ride with me and I will show you my island."

I was surprised at how I trusted this man, all of a sudden.

"I don't have time for sight seeing. I came to try and find my mother. I think she might be here. She used to live here."

"I know, I know. I hear all the news of the harbour, when people arrive, who they are. Do they have money? Are they alone? These people talk, talk, all day long." As he spoke he turned the key in the motorbike, dropped it off the stand and kicked the engine over. It roared as he turned the throttle.

"Will you come?" He raised his eyebrows. I stepped forward and swung my leg over the seat of the bike. I held on gently to his waist but he pulled my hands closer to him, patting them in place in front of him. We swung through the narrow streets before joining a road which took us away from the main town. The shops here were busy, local life continued despite the time of year. I realised how different it was from the harbour. I felt my body relax and my mind wander. I went back over my meeting with Karen. If she had mistaken this man for my father, he must resemble him. But then he's medium height and build, with thick dark hair, sharp features, not sharp exactly, quite fine in fact, a long nose which arches at the top. Like any of the local men. There is an arrogance about him which the other men don't have. I held tighter as our speed increased and leaned with him as we went around a corner. Something was familiar. That smell, that clear, chilled, earthy smell, like the cold, like my scarf, *like Christmas*, mum said.

I'm looking for a new place. I don't want to live in the harbour. It's never quiet. I scour the paper and attempt to decipher the adverts. I can read the script now but don't understand all the words, so I read aloud to Al and she translates for me. I have walked around the surrounding areas looking for the red and white signs which say ENOIKIAZETAI – FOR RENT, and found nothing. When Al's knowledge lets me down I turn to the dictionary and look up the words. We are chatting about words and the way they are pronounced. Put the emphasis on the wrong syllable or swap one letter and the sense is changed completely.

"*Pie-thakia, pe-thakia?*" *She offers.*

"*I know this one. Lamb chops, children.*"

"*Very good. How about psomee, psolee?*" *She's laughing so I know it's dirty.*

"*I know bread, go on tell me.*"

" *Bread and dick.*" *She is giggling like a schoolgirl.*

"*Hysterical. I'm trying to learn the language here. Right, a sensible one. Vroh-ki and vrok-ee, rain or trap.*"

My eye scans the page and falls on a word lower down, vrykolakas - vampire, spook, spectre.

We left the town, crossed the main highway and began climbing the mountain road. I closed my eyes and leaned into the bends with him as we danced up the hillside, like skaters on ice. Bending first one way then the other, rhythmically, effortlessly. As we slowed down, I opened my eyes to see a small taverna set back from the road. He led me to a table right on the edge of the mountainside, as I leaned on the wooden railing I could see the island stretching out before me. I looked across the groves of trees, the groups of houses, to the town, and at last the sea. He poured wine from a carafe on the table into two glasses and held his up to me.

"To Alithea."

I raised my glass to him in reply. "I don't know your name."

"They call me Xenon."

"Isn't that a gas?" I was being deliberately flippant.

"It means, stranger, outsider." I took a drink from the glass. The wine was dark and sweet, familiar.

"Tastes like village wine!" My mother's words that day in the restaurant back home. I noticed he didn't drink from his, but watched me closely, aware of every movement. It unsettled me, a feeling I wasn't used to, always so much in control, so measured.

Gesturing with his arm he said, "this is my land." I laughed and felt instantly more settled. He smiled, but his eyes fixed on me. He stretched out to touch me and leaned close.

"I have lived too long on this island, alone. The harbour crowd are fools, they come looking for solutions to their sorry little lives and the tourists drink themselves stupid on cheap alcohol. But you are different." I laughed again at this half hearted chat up line, but he held my arm tightly, his fingers pinching my skin, his face tightened and his voice deepened.

"I have watched you, I know you. You keep yourself apart from the rest. You are strong like me."

My head was aching again, I felt as if I was watching the scene from outside, this man holding me and speaking in hushed tones, declaring some kind of secret pact. A woman hovered at the table. To take their order, I supposed. He snapped at her to go. His face seemed to change, angular when he spoke to her, furrowed brows when he spoke to me again and then it softened as he relaxed his grip on my arm.

"I'm frightening you."

"Not at all. You don't frighten me." And I knew it was true. Suddenly I felt that he needed me and I was the one in control. For some reason he watched me, followed me even. He needed to be close, but I didn't believe that he meant me any harm at all. He gestured to the woman, and she returned with a plate piled high with prawns and cured meats, cheese, salad and bread.

"Can I have a beer? That wine's too strong for me, I'm not used to it."

"Of course," he inclined his head and called the woman back again. We ate in silence, I gazed out at the view, knowing he was watching me.

"I should get back." I stretched my arms above my head.

"Why hurry? Are you 'meeting someone' again?" Now he was laughing at me, his mood had lightened.

"Not today, no."

"Good." He lead me back to the motorbike. The air had a chill in it now, a light wind ran through the trees. I pulled my scarf out of my pocket and wrapped it around my neck. He slipped his fingers through my hair to lift it out from under the scarf and let his hand rest on my shoulder.

"Good," he said again and climbed onto the motorbike. I felt a shiver and leant into his back, tucking myself tightly behind him as we pulled away and onto the road. He turned the bike away from the town road and we continued to climb. I wished I'd eaten more, the taste of the wine mingled with the beer left an odd taste in my mouth. He turned off the road through an old stone gateway and

85

along a tree-lined track. I was sure this was the route that Doug had taken when we'd found the ruined house, but at the end of the track was a high wall. We drove through an archway and stopped just inside. I could see low outbuildings on either side of a paved yard and ahead was a house with a double flight of stairs to a front door. A few chickens ambled across the courtyard, clucking amiably. I felt sure I had been here before, seen this place before. Somewhere a dog barked. I pulled my jacket closer to me, tugged at the scarf. That smell again, sharp cold, mingled with earthy geranium and jasmine. He offered me his hand as we climbed the stairway to the front door. As we reached the top he turned to look at me.

"This is my home, Alithea. Welcome."

It is Ochi Day – huge celebrations for the day that Prime Minister Metaxa said 'No!' to Mussolini. While the local people attend parades in the towns, we ex-pats pack ourselves into cars and trucks and climb onto motorbikes and head out into the countryside to have a picnic. There is a real holiday atmosphere. We drive in convoy, laden down with beer, wine and food until we reach a village at the foot of the mountains which has a large field with a stream running to the side. We set up camp, fire up a barbecue, weigh down crates of beer in the stream along with the wine, to keep them cool.

We eat and drink and play rounders. Cries of 'drop the bat!' every time an American takes a turn. We try and explain it's not baseball. The ground is hard and dust kicks up as we run. Doug has taken charge of the barbecue, and a couple of English lads, Mark and Ken, set themselves up as barmen, making sure we are all served with ice cool beers, checking the ropes and rocks in the stream to make sure we don't lose any bottles to the current. There are four children in our party who are playing down by the trees out of the sun. I am lying watching and listening as they speak in a mixture of three different languages. A few more bikes arrive. We are a large group now, a family gathering. A family of misfits who have banded together here under the trees at the foot of the mountains to play games, drink a little, eat and relax after a long hard summer of work. The sun is dropping and three of the children have fallen asleep in the back of one of the pick-ups. Mark has had too much to drink.

"Come on, get in the car," Ken lays him on the back seat and tries to close the door. Mark mutters something and Ken replies,

"Never mind your bike for now."

"I'll drive it back," one of the lads on holiday offers. "I drive a motorbike at home."

I help Doug and Al pack up the food and crates and we

load it all into one of the trucks. The bikes set off and we arrange to meet them in the old kafeneon back in the harbour, for an evening drink, where we can sit and watch the sun drop off the horizon. The convoy weaves its way out of the field and back through the village towards the main road. We pass some of the mopeds.

"See you back at the harbour," we call out, beep our horn and wave. The larger bikes have gone on ahead, but as we round the corner Ken and the lad on Mark's bike have stopped. As we slow down to pass them, they shout to us.

"We're waiting for the papakis." 'Little duck' is the name the locals give to the small mopeds, because of the quacking sound the engine makes.

"We'll make sure they keep up."

They wave us on. We're in no rush. A few minutes later the bikes overtake again and drive ahead. We round a corner and they are waiting. They play this game as we drive home. We reach the junction with the Ethniki, the main road which cuts across the island from east to west, cross it and continue towards the town. Around the next sweeping corner, with the town almost in view, we see Ken waving at us.

The camber of the road is steep and the gulleys at either side of the road are deep. Ken's trials bike is dropped on its side, Mark's bike has slipped off the road. Doug pulls over and runs to see what's gone on. Ken is shaking, pacing up and down.

"It just flew at him, straight at him." He is muttering more to himself than to us. "Straight at him, bloody big black thing." I climb out to join Doug. The boy who'd been driving Mark's bike is lying at the side of the road, on his back, his arms at his side. The bike has skidded into the gulley without him. It lies, a huge beast of a thing, one wheel spinning.

"What happened?" Doug is shouting.

"A bird, I'm not sure," Ken still paces. I am walking towards the boy. No helmet, no leathers. I can hear the engine of the trials bike as it idles on its side. I call to Doug to switch it off. The noise is pulsing in my head and the cicadas are competing. I hear the papakis arrive behind us. More voices. Questions. Shouts. I hear, "ambulance,"

"telephone".

There are no houses close by, so no telephone. Alison is beside me now and we kneel next to the boy. His eyes are closed. He has gravel across the side of his face. A dog is barking. Alison stands up,

"Thank god," she cries. A pick–up truck pulls across the road in front of us and a man steps out. It is Korakas. He shouts to Doug and the others to help lift the boy.

"No!" shouts Doug, "you fool, don't move him. We have to get a medic."

"There are no medics here!" Korakas hisses at him. "Do as I say." And they do. They lift the boy and gently lay him in the back of the truck. Korakas takes my elbow and leads me towards it.

"Go with him. Hold him"

I climb up and hold his head to stop it rolling as we set off. I steady it as we drive over dirt and drop into pot-holes. The dust flies up on either side. My shoulders have burned and are tightening now. I hold his head and look at the shape of his face, his lips, his eyelids. His hair has stuck to the grazing at his temple, black with blood and sweat. I try to remember what colour his eyes are, what his voice sounds like.

"Drop the bat! Drop the bat!"

I am cradling a dead boy in the back of a truck in a strange country and I feel nothing. I do not know his name.

I strode up to the table where Alison sat reading her newspaper. "I met Karen."

"Oh great!" Said Alison, without looking up.

"Don't be like that," warned Doug.

"And why not?" She snapped. "That woman."

"Who was always so good to Anna," Doug reminded her.

"So what's wrong with her?" I asked, petulantly. Doug raised his eyebrows and pulled Alison's paper down enough to look at her over the top,

"Well?"

"She's a flake. She talks to animals for goodness sake." She shook her paper straight again, "Invisible ones."

"She said we were neighbours when I was little."

"Yeah, you were," Doug took over. "She was great. Looked out for you both. She lived close and we couldn't get near without him catching on."

"Why?"

"In the winter the roads up near the house were pretty bad. You needed a decent truck to get out there. Mud all over, bits of tree in the way. Snow, one year. She could walk and see you, we had to borrow a truck, that made it tricky, we had to plan it, couldn't just drop by." He raised his hand to call the waiter over and ordered another coffee.

"I can't stop." I looked back across my shoulder towards the square where a few cars were parked up.

"Oh?" Alison looked over her paper, folded it carefully and lay it on the table. "Why the hurry?"

As if in response we heard, "Alithea!" A man stood by one of the trucks in the square and raised his arm.

I darted back through the tables, calling back to them,
"I'll see you."

*

"Jesus! Was that?" Said Doug.

"Was that who?" Alison replied angrily.

"Was that Korakas?"

"For Christ's sake Doug, nobody's seen him for years now. Give it up will you?"

As the truck drove past the kafeneon and along the waterfront, Doug could see Ally talking animatedly to the driver, she laid her head on his shoulder for a moment, so Doug got a clear sight of the driver. The man had a streak of white through his thick hair, his face was lined and dark, his features sharp.

"Did you see? Did you see him? Al..." But Alison picked up her paper, folded it back to the crossword page and said nothing.

I am lying on a narrow couch and thinking about that boy in the hospital. How Korakas summoned them all to him. How they ran to do just what he told them without question. They lifted the boy and laid him on a trolley, wheeled him away from me, through the hospital doors. I knew that he was dead and wanted to tell them it was too late. Korakas took my hands in his and helped me down from the truck, then held me close-in to his chest as we walked. Like my father held me the time we had the dog put down when I was twelve. His arms encompassed me and I could smell that cold aroma which seems to accompany him.

And I realise I can smell it now. He is watching me. On a chair in the corner of the room he sits and watches me. He smiles. As he does, his features soften. I shiver. I look down to see if I am wearing my clothes. I am, with a soft blanket thrown over me.

"Are you afraid I had molested you?" He is mocking me. I do not answer. He can read my mind.

"Anna, you are special to me. You must know this."
I want to ask where I am, but that seems foolish. I want to ask what time it is, what day it is. I can see the reddish glow of the sky through the window behind him, but not the sun itself. The light is soft and he seems younger than when I last saw him. Last time he seemed taller and harder. I remember the feeling of his arms around me, the strength in them. They protect me like a cloak. I feel delicate, precious. I know he would guard me from the harm out there in the darkness. Hadn't he done it already, at the beach, in the alley that night and now with that boy on the road?

"Come, let's eat."
He takes my hands again and pulls me to my feet, the blanket falling to the floor. It is soft, woven from some thread with long fibres, dark green, almost black. Outside the door is a balcony running the

92

length of the small town-house. We descend the stone steps into a courtyard with a gate onto the street. He has a motorbike parked on the pavement and leads me to it. I hesitate, pulling back on his hand.

"I am a careful driver. You will be safe with me."

He climbs on confidently and drops it off the stand. I wait until he starts it and climb behind him. As we drive through the streets I lean into his back and breathe in the scent of him. It is the smell of cold air rushing into a warm house on a winter day. My father standing in the doorway at Christmas, stamping his feet to shake off snow. We leave the town, cross the Ethniki and begin climbing the mountain road. I close my eyes and lean into the bends with him as we dance up the hillside, like skaters on ice. Bending first one way then the other, rhythmically, effortlessly. Now I open them as we stop at a small taverna set back from the road. We sit at a table right on the edge of the mountainside and below the whole island stretches before us. I can see across the groves of trees, the groups of houses, the town, lit up now, to the sea. He pours wine from a carafe on the table into two glasses and holds his up to me.

"To Anna."

I drink from my glass, the wine is dark and sweet. He doesn't drink from his. He watches me intently and I am aware of every movement I make. Gesturing with his arm he says,

"all this is mine."

I find myself laughing at him,

"you sound like the devil tempting Christ!"

He smiles, but his eyes do not waver, holding mine in their gaze. He grabs my forearms and leans in towards me.

"Anna. I have lived on this island for many years. The locals are jealous, inbred fools. The foreigners come looking for solutions to their sorry little lives and the tourists drink themselves stupid on cheap alcohol. Then every once in a while comes a girl like you."

I begin to protest, but he holds me tighter.

"I have watched you, in the village, in the town, surrounded by the people you call your friends. I know you. You have an old spirit, you keep yourself apart from the rest. You are strong like me." A woman is hovering at our table, he snaps at her to go. His face changes in the light, angular when he speaks to her, furrowed brows when he speaks to me and then it softens as he relaxes his grip on my arms.

"I'm frightening you." I remember the look on Nikos' face, that boy across the street. I remember what he did with those men in the alley that night with Doug. He gestures to the woman, and she returns with a meze, a platter piled high with prawns and cured meats, cheese, salad and bread. We eat and we talk, of ordinary things, the island, the weather, the ducks on the beach, village life and life in the town. He makes me laugh with stories of foolish old women, like Chrissoula, and their superstitions. The sun has dropped right behind the horizon and the sky is almost black. There are no street-lights here. The lights in the town trace pathways into the darkness around it and I imagine our route back down the mountain all the way home to the harbour. Finally he gestures to the woman, makes a signature in the air and she returns with a plate of watermelon and refuses to take payment for the meal. He nods at her but leaves several notes on the table as he stands up, offering his hand to me. I put my hand in his and he leads me to the motorbike.

"You are cold." From the pannier he pulls a shawl, soft and dark, like the blanket he had laid over me before, and drops it onto my shoulders. I do feel cold but I am not sure if it is the night air which makes me feel this way. Instead of riding back down the mountainside, we continue to climb. I can taste the wine and I can smell him as I lean closer, tired now.

He turns off the road through an old stone gateway and along a tree-lined track. At the end of the track is a high wall. He drives through an archway, stopping just inside. Low outbuildings flank the paved courtyard and ahead of us is a house with a double flight of stairs to a front door. I look up to the sky. No cloud cover, clear and dark, painted with stars. Somewhere a dog barks. I pull the shawl around me and smell that odour of him, sharp cold, mingled with earthy geranium and night flowering jasmine. I stumble a little and he throws his arm around me as we climb the stairway to the front door. As we reach the top he lifts my chin with his hand and looks down at me. "This is my home, Anna. Welcome."

"Let's just go home." I lay my head against the back of the seat, closed my eyes and listened to the sound of the engine.

"Home?" He smiled and glanced across at me. "My home?"

"Yeah." I didn't move, or open my eyes, but I knew that he was watching me, glancing at me as we drove through the town.

"I'm sick of the harbour. Same people, same thing every day. No wonder mum left, I reckon she got sick of that lot."

The truck accelerated as we left the town and joined the Ethniki. After a few minutes we turned again, leaving the main road. I kept my eyes closed and tried to judge where we were. The sound of the gears, the feel of the road, I reckoned we were climbing as the truck was in a low gear now, and the road wound this way and that. Houses. I could hear a dog barking, so there must be houses. Other cars passing. The truck slowed and came to a standstill. I felt Xenon's hand on my shoulder. A firm grip. Strong.

"We're here."

I opened my eyes to see we were in a village square.

"I thought you were taking me home?"

"No. First we will eat."

"You lot do nothing but eat."

As we crossed the square, heading for the taverna, two big, black birds squabbled over a piece of discarded food. Xenon kicked out at them.

"Fige!" He snarled. They lifted themselves into the air with a few effortless beats of their wings. I put my hand in his, allowing myself to be lead like a child. He seemed irritated, turning his head to look, first in one direction then the other, as if he had lost somebody. I could feel every bone in his hand as it wrapped around mine. He felt cold.

95

The owner of the taverna made a great show of greeting us. Much back slapping and hand shaking, then bowed slightly and showed us inside. He sat us at a table near the back and called to his wife to bring wine and bread, some olives. When this was done he called us through into the shop at the side of the taverna, which I discovered was a butcher's. In the corner was a large stainless steel cold store. He threw the door of this open and called us to look inside.

"You choose," said Xenon. "What will you eat?" The meat hung around me, pork and beef, half a lamb.

"No, I really don't mind. You chose."

Xenon spoke to the man, pointing at this joint and that one. The butcher deftly cut selected pieces of meat, slicing a kidney from a carcass, some small lamb chops, some pork. He held a lamb's heart in his hand and laughed, pointed to Xenon and said something. Xenon laughed back.

"What did he say?" I asked.

"He says I should take the heart of a lamb, because I don't have one of my own."

"And do you?"

"Of course. I have a heart which is capable of loving beyond the capacity of an ordinary man."

I laughed, but he looked very serious.

"Don't disapprove of me." I said, reaching to touch him. I realised I needed his approval very much.

"I don't disapprove. But I am disappointed when you don't understand me."

"I'm sorry."

"I need you to understand me. You are special to me."

I wanted to laugh again. When he spoke like that it made me feel uneasy. I was distracted by a woman's voice, raised. Across the room an old village woman crossed herself. The man with her pulled her hand roughly down to stop her. He whispered in her ear and she shrieked something back at him, pushing her chair back and standing up quickly. I heard the word, 'pamay' which I know means let's go. The man tried to reason with the old woman, but she would have nothing to do with him. She walked past me and as she did she dropped something onto the table in front of me. Xenon lifted himself slightly from his seat and bowed his head to the woman,

"kalinichta yiayia."

The woman crossed herself and left. I looked down at the table to see a tiny glass bead on a gold safety pin, bright blue with a black centre, like a bright eye. I picked it up to see it more closely.

"I had one of these when I was little."

"Stupid old women. They make me crazy."

"What is it?"

"To ward off the eye. The evil eye," he explained.

"Crossing herself and trusting to these?" I held the bead between my fingers. "Nothing like hedging your bets! What have you done to deserve that kind of reaction?"

"I told you, these people are stupid. I'm an outsider."

I wanted to lighten his mood.

"Come on, let's eat. I don't want my night spoiled by a stupid old woman."

He leant forward and took my hand, shaking the bead from it. He bent down and kissed the palm.

"Yes, let's eat."

I woke up late again this morning. The sun is filtering through the old shutters, casting a slanted shadow on the far wall. Ants are crawling across the plate on the floor. One has climbed into the tumbler and drowned in the residue of the sticky wine we were drinking last night. I can hear Korakas downstairs and smell coffee. I find myself developing a liking for the treacle he serves up. I find myself developing a liking for a lot of things he does. I close my eyes and think of the way he moves, the way he talks and how he watches me. The smell of coffee has mingled with that fresh smell he has about him, like cold rushing into a warm room. I open my eyes and he is standing over me, watching.

"What's your name?" I ask him.

"You know it. They call me Korakas." He dismisses the question as he often does and takes me by the hand, pulling me to my feet. "Come, let's take breakfast."

In the kitchen he pulls out a chair for me and pushes a cup of coffee across the table. There is fruit and a hard cheese and bread, which is still warm.

"Where's the bakery?" I ask.

"I will bring you bread. I will feed you." *He is laughing at me.* "You need do nothing. You have me now."

I have no idea how far we are from the town, or the nearest village. I haven't left the house for days. I'm not even sure how many days. My clothes are hanging in a cupboard upstairs and I keep forgetting to ask how they got there. The accident is a vague memory. I wonder how they contacted the boy's family? Korakas dealt with the police at the hospital and it was there I last saw Doug and Alison.

"Did they bring my brown bag when they brought my things?"

"They?" He glares at me. His eyebrows pulling together like plumage on the face of a hawk.

"Doug and Alison, didn't they bring my things?"

"I dealt with it." He pushes the chair backwards, almost toppling it and moves to the door. "You don't need their help."

"They're my friends." I feel suddenly afraid. I don't know anything about this man and I am alone in his house, with no way of finding my way back home.

"This is your home now," as if he had read my thoughts. He sweeps back towards me and drops to his knees in front of me, holding my hands in my lap. "I need you Anna. I need you." His eyes plead with me and he drops his head. I stroke his hair. It is dark and soft, a little coarser at the sides then at the nape of his neck it is like down. I feel him push his head against my hand and flex the muscles in his neck, then he looks up at me again.

"Come," he stands up and pulls me to my feet. "Today I will show you some of the island. Go and get dressed." He taps me on my behind as I run past him and go upstairs to the bedroom. The room is bare, but for the large bed, an old cupboard where my clothes hang and a table in front of the window with a chair at its side. The window is framed by jasmine and looks out onto a small walled garden. My few bits of jewellery, toiletries and hairbrush have been arranged on the table. I drag the brush through my hair quickly and wonder again who brought my things here and who laid them out so neatly.

"Anna!" He calls up the stairs. I pull on a dress I bought from a stall in the harbour, one of the girls brings stuff in from Thailand – bright colours printed on soft cotton, a long flowing skirt to keep the sun from burning my legs in the height of the summer. I realise that I may be cold if we stay out all day and reach out to grab my jeans from the chair.

"No. Wear the dress." I turn to see him standing in the doorway, watching again.

"I'll get cold later on." I begin, but he interrupts.

"Wear the dress." He turns and walks downstairs, leaving me alone in the bedroom.

It was dark by the time we reached the house. There were no street lights to cast an orange glow across the sky out here. As we climbed the steps Xenon glanced back, as if he had seen something.

"What's the matter?" I asked.

"Nothing at all." He held my arm tightly and steered me up the steps and into the house.

"I'll make some coffee," I said and went through the motions I had watched as a child, spooning coffee into the briki, stirring carefully. Don't break the waves, I heard my mother's voice. He cried out and I turned to see what was wrong. He stood, his chair lay on its side, where he had kicked it back to stand up.

"You cannot stay here tonight. I will take you back."

"What do you mean? Take me back?" I dropped the briki and the coffee spilled over the stove, killing the flame, and dripped to the floor, leaving a dark stain on the tiles at my feet. He stepped forward and turned off the gas, then took my hands in his.

"Ela moraki, I cannot keep you here tonight."

"Make your mind up! One minute you're seducing me and the next you're cooing at me, like I'm a baby."

"Don't be angry with me. You are both to me. You are special."

"Save it will you? We both know what we're up to here."

He tightened his grip on my hands, pulling me close to him.

"Don't ever cheapen yourself in that way. Do you hear?"

I could feel his body against mine, feel his strength. I was alone up here, a long way from the harbour, I had no idea exactly where. It was dark outside and cold. He relaxed his grip a little and I felt his warmth, could smell that odour, fresh and sharp. I wanted to tell him what a jerk he was, I wanted to lean against him and feel his arms tighten around me, I wanted to cry and I wanted my mother.

As suddenly as he had grabbed me, he let me go, then cupped my head in his hands and kissed me lightly on the lips. I clenched my teeth and fought the impulse to cry. I never cried. "Fine, take me back then." Like a petulant child I pulled away from him and walked out of the door, hoping that he would call me back. I heard him slam the door as he followed me down the stone steps into the courtyard.

I love to hold him. I lie against his back and turn my head to the side as the bike pulls out through the gates and we ride down the track to the road. I trust him, I know I'll be safe as long as I lean with him and keep close. Today we head towards town, but then turn along the Ethniki in the opposite direction. I breathe in his smell and smile. The road is wide and winds between the houses and trees. The breeze is still warm although it must be nearing the end of October now. He pulls over and parks beneath a huge tree, an oak I think. He leads me to a table and beckons to the old woman sitting in the shade. She shuffles over to us and grunts a greeting, forcing a smile for me. A tourist car is parked to one side and I notice a man and a woman come out of a small church on the opposite side of the road, just on the bend. She is clutching a guide book, waving it in the air as she talks to the man. They cross the road and choose a table. They are English. Unmistakeable, in shorts and sandals. Each carries a small backpack. The old woman bustles over to them, making a great show of welcoming them. A boy brings us a meze and a beer, with two glasses. I pick at the food, some cheese, large prawns, lumps of meat. I try one, it is strong and dark and chewy.

"What's this? Dried camel?" I screw up my face in disgust. He laughs at me and touches my hand lightly.

"Here," he leans across and puts a peeled prawn in my mouth.

"Excuse me." The English woman calls across to us. I open my mouth to answer, but he squeezes my hand and rises from his chair. He inclines his head in a bow and replies,

"Madam?"

The woman blushes slightly, "we'd like to order one of those, what is it?" She points to the plate of food. Her husband sighs loudly.

"Leave it to me." Korakas calls the old woman over and

orders for them. She shuffles away.

"A meze, madam." He explains to her.

"Here if you order an ouzo it will be accompanied by a small plate of food, some bread, some olives, perhaps some cheese. When you order your second drink, the plate will grow, a third, even more food. It is not good to drink without food." He raises his glass to the couple, inclines his head again, "stin iyia sas."

Skinny arses, I think to myself, remembering the fun we had at Al's making up English phrases for the local words. Lorry Gary gizmo, park your load – to logariasmo parakalo - the bill please. I wonder what they are doing now? Sitting together in the harbour, reading bits from the paper, sharing the crossword. I feel suddenly lonely.

"Oh, yes, yar -mass," the woman stumbles over the word from her phrase book, "cheers." Her husband glowers at Korakas, who takes his seat again, but this time next to me. He puts his arm around the back of my chair and rests his hand on my shoulder.

"We've been to the church," the woman continues. "We saw the altar, so sad." Korakas's fingers flex involuntarily against me.

"Sad?" He spits the word out. "Such destruction, sad?"

"I think my wife," the man speaks for the first time, "I think my wife and I struggle to find the right words in the face of such a monument."

Korakas relaxes. The old village woman begins to gabble away at the couple, she holds out a wooden frame to the man, talking all the while. She crosses over to me and waves it at me, then rests in on the table. It is a yellowed letter in a simple wooden picture frame. A royal crest at the top, then a brief type written note thanking, her I presume, for assistance during the war. From the pocket of her apron she produces a folded telegram, well worn, thanking her for aiding the escape of two British Airman. As she speaks in a broken language, she drops into a chair at our table. Words I don't understand, then some English, then some German. Her eyes fill with tears and slowly one finds its way down her cheek, running the course of her wrinkled face. Her hand tightens on the telegram and bangs against her thigh, again and again and her voice rises. Korakas drops to his knees and grabs her fist to prevent it *from banging again.*

"Shh, yiayia." He strokes the top of her arm.

"Oh, I'm so sorry," says the English woman. The boy comes out of the kitchen and throws up his head in acknowledgement at Korakas as he leads his grandmother back inside. She pulls away from him and turns to speak again. I don't understand what she says, her look towards Korakas has softened, and yet it sounds as if she is uttering some kind of incantation. I understand 'kopella' and 'pethi'- girl and child and I know she is talking about me. He nods at her and smiles.

"I want to see inside the church," I stand up.

"Anna, let's go." But I cross the road and run towards the small building. Inside it is very quiet and cool. The bare walls have small windows in them. There is a shrine with a lamp burning in it and flowers at its base and in the centre of the space is a stone altar with glass sides. It seems to be full of stones, but as I walk towards it I see that the stones are skulls, and each skull has a hole right through it.

"Bullet holes. Nazi bullets" Korakas is beside me. "The skulls of villagers, Resistance fighters, innocents who would not supply information." He lays his hand on the top stone and I hear him whisper, "my people".

I stood in the small booth in the gift shop, telephone receiver pressed against my ear. The familiar ringing tone sounded so out of place here in the sunshine, like a pop song at a funeral. I felt conspicuous. It rang and rang, no reply. I imagined the house, quiet, the kitchen still holding the secret of whatever had gone on with my mother. I felt like I'd been away for months and yet it was hardly a week. I realised that a young girl was waiting to use the telephone so I hung up. The connection severed, I felt sick and pushed past the other customers to get outside. A hand touched my arm and I pulled away, but then realised it was the young girl offering me the phone card I had left in the telephone. I was jumpy. It was hard to find anywhere in this town where you could sit undisturbed. I felt watched all the time. If it wasn't Xenon turning up, it was Doug or Alison, or even that woman Karen. Part of me could see the attraction this island had for people, but part of me rejected it. Narrow- minded people, the locals and the incomers. I wondered what held people here, kept them from moving on.

Trying to put space between me and the already familiar cafés and bars, I walked the length of the harbour towards the town beach, a sad strip of sand which was packed with tourists. If I was a painter, I could capture the light as it reflected off the sea. Perhaps not, perhaps there was no way of capturing the essence of this place. An old man sat unravelling nets on a fishing boat moored at the sea wall. Two small children were playing in a shabby park on the corner, one on a swing and the other on a rusty climbing frame. The earth was hard and dry, a remnant of what must have been grass at one time. The children called out to each other. The old man looked up from his work and smiled at me. Just past the park I sat on a bench and looked out to sea. Some way out was an island.

I shaded my eyes against the sun, to take a better look. The old man called something to me, he was pointing and talking, as if telling me a story. He called to a younger man sitting astride a Vespa and gesticulated towards me. The young man strolled across.

"He says to beware Ketos."

"Oh?"

"The monster, look," he pointed to the island.

"Ketos was sent to destroy our island and our people. See the huge mouth, with teeth?"

The island protruded from the waves like an ungainly, lumpen beast. At the west side the cliff face was eroded into a large cave, which, if you stretched your imagination, did look like gaping jaws.

"The Kraken?" I remembered my mother's stories.

"Ketos we say. Turned to stone. But some nights he will move, look again tomorrow and see if he is in the same place. Beware, he keeps those here who wish to flee." The man laughed. "It's what the old people say."

"I thought this was paradise and you all wanted to stay?"

He looked serious for a moment. "You are a tourist?"

"I was born here."

"And you come back. It is not just Ketos who keeps us here. We are born here, we live here, we eat and breathe this island. Without it we are nothing."

"Blimey." I raised my eyebrows dismissively, weary of the constant story telling these people indulged in. The man shrugged. I watched as he walked back to his motorbike. I reckoned him to be about thirty years old, in work clothes, a builder maybe? And yet he spoke English far better than I could speak French and I'd studied that since I was eleven. And how did he know I spoke English? It was if they were attuned to the visitors and knew just what language to speak and what to speak about. He raised his hand as he drove past, back towards the harbour, and I waved in reply.

"It's just a lump of rock."

"Talking to yourself?" Xenon was leaning on the wall a few feet away from me. I hadn't seen him since he'd dropped me back at my room that night. He had been silent for the whole drive.

"Creeping up on young women, as usual?"

"Alithea, are you still angry with me?"

"Why would I be angry?"

"You seemed so, the other night. That is why I have left you alone."

"But you always know where to find me."

"Of course, I see everything, and what I do not see, they tell me," he swept his hand towards the trees where three large black birds sat, sullenly looking out across the water, watching.

"There you go again, so creepy." I laughed and walked away.

"Creepy?" He called after me and I turned back to look at him.

"You know, weird? Dark?" I began to walk backwards, slowly, a step at a time, coaxing him to follow.

"Yes, dark. I am dark," he began to walk towards me.

"See? That's creepy."

"And yet, you are not afraid."

I turned around, began to walk on and said, "My mother taught me not to show fear," glancing over my shoulder at him. He stood still, not watching me now. I stopped, I'd lost him again.

"Hey, what did I say?" I heard the toot of a motorcycle horn and the driver called out to me.

"Beware the monsters," the man on his Vespa, coming back from the direction of the harbour, a bag of shopping at his feet. Laughing, he waved at me. I turned back to Xenon, but he had gone. I thought I could see him walking down one of the narrow streets away from the sea, but as I followed I realised it was an older man, slightly bent and walking too slowly, so I turned again and continued to walk the length of the beach.

Since that last trip he has been so quiet. No stories or tales of the history of this place. We spend time together, just us. I fall asleep next to him and when I wake he is already gone from the bed. He sleeps very little. Sometimes I watch him as he sits in a chair under the tree in the courtyard, head thrown back, eyes closed. If I move, he opens them and smiles at me, stretches out his hand to touch mine.

This morning I wake to find myself alone in the bed. There are no sounds from the kitchen below. I pull on a t-shirt to go downstairs, trailing my hand on the wooden banister as I go. The stairs are as worn as the handrail and I wonder how many feet have trodden up and down and who they belonged to. The kitchen is empty, the back door open. It is unusual for me to be alone in the house. This sudden freedom from his watch makes me feel trapped. He watches me eat and sleep, dress and undress. He watches me shower and bathe. Although I have never wanted to be away from him I feel sure that if I did he would not allow it. I know that we are halfway up the mountain, but I have no idea what the place is called, or where the nearest village is, the nearest neighbour. Something startles the chickens outside. A truck is pulling away and he stands one arm raised to the driver. He calls out to the man, who leans on his horn in response. Laughing he walks through the gateway and across the yard towards the house. Seeing me, he runs up the stone steps and pulls me to him, his hand at the back of my neck, cupping my head.

"Anna." He steers me towards the table and I sit in the chair. From a crumpled up supermarket bag he produces a tiny golden plum and offers it to me. It smells of honey, not honey, it smells of, something else.

"Eat it," he says, as he tears it apart and offers me the flesh. The fruit tastes like the sweetest plum, small, slippery, like mango or

passion fruit. "Despila, from a tree on my land in the mountains."
Inside are three flat sided stones, he holds them in the palm of his
hand. "These stones symbolise our family. Father, mother and child,
yet to be born." I am embarrassed but pleased. He speaks such crap
sometimes but it makes me feel great. I amaze myself how I lap it
all up. And a child, why not? I never saw the tree, I never saw him
pick the fruit, but he would bring me a bag as a treat and I would eat
them as greedily as a child eats sweets.

I woke with a new clarity. I needed help. That guy Xenon kept distracting me, taking me off, stopping me from looking for mum. Besides he just confused me. My few exploits with boys of my own age didn't compare to how I felt when I was with Xenon. One minute I felt a heat between us that pulled at me and the next I wanted to crawl into his arms to be held like a child. I had been excited and afraid when we went to his house in the mountains. He kept leading me on, then pushing me away, and all that crap about cheapening myself made me angry. Mum was right, these men lived by such double standards, a girl had to be pure as the driven snow or she was nothing. What did he want from me then? That wasn't clear at all.

Resolved to do something positive and not let this creeping apathy drag me off track, I set out for the harbourfront to look for Doug or Alison. Instead of heading straight to the waterfront I turned up through the back streets intending to cut across to the cafés on the far side. I found myself heading up the street and came out into a courtyard, a square with a tree and a sorry-looking climbing frame in the centre. The doors around the square were locked-up, signs swinging in the breeze above each door, naming the tavernas which must be packed in the evenings. I imagined the tables filled with tourists, waiters scuttling in between, although nobody rushed here, I'd had to get used to that. I wasn't sure which way to go now. A road ran behind the square, it climbed upwards, away, I presumed, from the harbourfront. So I walked down the narrow road and came to the busy street which had been lined with traders when I'd first arrived.

As I stopped to wait for a taxi to go past, I caught sight of a woman across the street, a scarf tied around her hair. She slipped down the street hung with leather of all descriptions and disappeared out of sight. I ran across the street between the cars which followed on behind the taxi. Wanting to shout out, but finding that the sound wouldn't come out. A driver shouted at me through an open car window. I chased along the street, ducking under the low hanging wares outside the shops, dodging around shoppers ambling along in my way. I'd lost her. I had been sure for a moment, the way the woman moved, the long stride, the tilt of her head, I had been sure it was my mother.

The street gave way to a road which ran down to the harbour front again or up to the town centre. Aimlessly I wandered across the road, looking either way to see if I could catch sight of her again. I felt a tightening in my throat, I could feel my pulse in my chest, in my temples, increasing, faster and stronger. Traffic was heavier here, the streets linking to the main town roads which lead out to the peninsula and up to the Ethniki, the main road, which runs across the island, east to west. Further on a few traders had laid out rugs with various wares on them, I walked past hardly noticing the cheap handbags, watches and shoes. At the end of this street the road turned back down towards the harbour and here the weekly market was set up. Women dressed in black, pulling baskets on wheels, walked between the stalls pinching and plucking at fruit and vegetables, poking chickens in crates, smelling herbs. I followed them, taking in the odours, the colours, the sounds. Languages I couldn't understand, local people, incomers, calling to each other, bargaining, arguing, laughing. I looked at every face, watched every gesture for one which was familiar. The posture, the stride, the ease with which she moved through a crowd. A woman banged into me and cursed, an old man thrust a slice of cheese at me to taste, the stench of rotting vegetables hit my nostrils as I tripped on a bag of rubbish left at the side of the street. I was confused and turned sharply to find a way out and walked straight into somebody. I looked up to apologise and smelled that earthy smell I had become accustomed to.

"Alithea. Are you alright?" I leaned against him and felt that surge of anger at him and at myself.

"I saw my mother." His eyes flicked from side to side as if

recording every aspect of the street.

"No, this is not possible." He looked again across the stalls and up to the trees, where a large bird launched itself across the heads of the traders and off towards the mountains. "You are unwell," he held my arm and as he did I felt my legs give way beneath me. "This place can affect you in this way. You walk the streets, you breathe in this air. Things are not always as they appear."

"I saw a woman."

"Come, we shall see if we can find this woman." He stroked my face and slipped his arm around my waist. I felt weak and leaned in to him, half supported.

"I can't think when I'm with you. You need to leave me alone. I can't do this with you. I can't think clearly with you."

"Am I so intoxicating? Come with me, come and rest. You are upset. It is close here in the market and the streets have made you confused. Sometimes the streets can make you a little crazy, you are far from the places that you know."

I let him lead me through back streets into an alleyway, where he sat me down at a small table outside a kafeneon. I sat with my back to the wall and rested my head against the cold stone, my eyes closed. He disappeared for a moment and returned with two glasses of tsikouthia.

"Here, drink this." He put the glass into my hand and raised it to my lips for me. I inhaled the familiar odour of currants and sipped slowly. The liquid warmed my throat and hit my stomach.

"I'm sorry," I said quietly. "I must seem a little strange."

"To lose a parent is hard. I understand this."

"She's not dead."

"Of course. I understand." I sat quietly and sipped some more of the drink.

"I too never knew my father," his voice comforted me and I closed my eyes and listened, "only stories about his skill and craftsmanship, tainted by the bitterness my mother felt because of the role he played in my brother's death. And I lost my mother too. She was lost to me even while she was alive. When my brother died nothing would console her, so I tried as hard as I could to make her happy. I gave my life to her and yet this was not enough. I sacrificed my childhood for her and yet this was not enough."

His history echoed mine. I had never known my father, I had lost part of my childhood just like him, I had lost my mother for days at a time long before she had disappeared from the house, lost her to her obsession about the birds and the trees and the threat of the sea. I let the tears come, there at a table in the street, I allowed myself to cry, for all the times I had held it back. I let my head rest against the ancient stone wall behind me, with my eyes closed and cried. Xenon watched and smiled.

Days are not so warm now. He is away for longer periods and leaves me alone. He has an old TV in the room next to the kitchen, I watch re-runs of American soaps and read the subtitles in an effort to learn the language, matching the words I know, to the symbols which make up the script. On the local channels they show puppet shows every morning, strange shadow puppets acting out folk tales. One character is a great bird who swoops down and captures a princess. The narrator gabbles away, but I understand none of it.

"Why do you watch this shit all day?" He often surprises me like that, creeping up on me when I least expect it.

"I thought you'd gone for the day," I hold my hand out to him. I want to draw him close because he seems angry. "Where did you go?"

"To the harbour." His speech is coarse and clipped. There is none of the softness he usually reserves for me.

"I would have gone with you. I'm lonely here. Besides, it's been ages since I've seen my friends."

"Your friends? What friends? Those harbour girls you used to hang around with and the boys? They're not friends. Once you've dropped out for a while they forget quickly enough."

"Hang on…"

"Turn that thing off!" He marches past me and slams his hand against the TV to switch it off.

"These village tales make me crazy! You want to know the real story?" He turns away and walks into the kitchen. I follow him and watch as he begins to prepare coffee. I take the briki from him and go through the process, spooning the powder into the small pan of water, adding sugar then stirring it slowly as it rises on the heat. Lift it off gently just as the foam reaches a head, just before it breaks. I pour the thick coffee into a cup for him. He takes it from me and touches my hand, gentle again. He smiles and his voice softens. "Anna." He sets the cup on the table and sits on the old wooden chair at its side. He reaches out for me, taking me by the hips and pushes me against the table in front of him. He pushes his face into my belly and breathes in deeply. I feel light in his grasp, as his hands seem to circle my entire body. Enclosed, but supported.

"I would like to go in one day with you." I try again. He rocks me lightly, and I close my eyes. "Just for a while," I whisper. "To catch up with everyone."

He looks up at me, keeping his hands firmly around me, and speaks quietly.

"I am the black bird and I see everything! You are the woman who I have chosen, with your golden hair and eyes like roasted almond, you are the princess now and you must stay. There is no going back from this point. I watch you. I know your every move, your thoughts. I know that you are tiring of me and want to leave. Well I'll tell you this now! You shall not leave! You have nowhere to go. Stay with me and I will make you happy. I will give you everything. Leave and I will send my people to find you and I will bring you back. I will always bring you back."

His hands tighten around my hips, fingers digging into me. His eyes are small and hard. As I look down at him his face becomes sharp and his features change. I don't understand the words. His face is dark and repugnant. He pulls himself upright, still grasping me tightly. He towers above me now and all I can see is the blackness of his chest and smell that earthy odour. He pulls me in to him, enfolds me in blackness and still I can feel his grip.

"You're hurting me!" I cry out and try to pull away. "You're scaring me! Let go!"

He recoils, from himself. His face softens, his hands fall to his sides and I step back but find myself trapped between him and the table. I sit back on it, try and relax. I feel the wood, solid and real, a table. I look at him but I don't know what he is anymore. How stupid I am. I'm here alone and know nothing about him. He runs his hand across his face as if wiping it clean and then through his thick black hair. As he does, something falls from his hand and I watch as it drifts to the table. Carefully I put my hand over it, because I know he did not see it fall. I close my fingers around it and bring both hands up to my chest and rest my chin on them. I feel his hand rest for a moment on top of my head before he leaves the room. I keep my eyes closed. I hear a chicken squawk, some flapping, then those damn birds in the trees beyond the courtyard. I open my eyes to see where he is, but he's gone. I open my hand and see a greenish black feather, pressed against my palm.

"I need your help." I pulled my chair closer to the table and leant towards Doug.

"You know I'd do anything to help you." He sipped his coffee noisily and smiled at me. It reminded me of the way mum drinks coffee.

"I know my mother must have come here, but how come nobody's seen her?"

"Alithea, baby," Doug hesitated, "I can't believe your mom would have come back here, I told you."

"But where else would she go?"

"I don't know honey, and I'm pretty sure she wouldn't leave you unless she had to."

"So help me find out where she is."

"Al knows some girls out at the airport, maybe they could check back through the passenger manifests, see if she flew in. If she came by boat we've no way of knowing."

"It's a start." I paused, "wouldn't she come straight to her friends if she came back?"

"Not if she came to see your father, she'd know I'd try and stop her."

"And why is that? Eh Doug? My father the king of the bogey men? King of the crows?"

"Don't joke about him."

"He spies on us, sends the birds to watch us, the clockwork crows, hopping along the path and cawing in the trees. They tell him where we are and if we venture too close to the sea he will lure us back across the water to him – and once he has us here we can never leave. The king who can never leave these shores and needs his princess to rule with him or he will wither and grow old, but

117

never die! I know the stupid stories."

"Then I'll tell you the truth," a shadow fell across the table. Alison stood, her hand shading her eyes from the sun. "I'll tell you the truth."

"Alison, honey,"

"Doug! Enough of the stories now, let me speak."

"Tell me then," I said.

"She would never say a word against him, she said he loved her, and he loved you, but he wouldn't let either of you breathe. She couldn't go out, couldn't have visitors, couldn't laugh or sing unless it was for him, he took a bright, funny girl and turned her into someone afraid. I never saw him raise a hand to her, or you, but he told her stuff, his stories, he made her believe he had power over her. And you," she swung round to Doug, "like a fool you fuelled it, played along with the stupid game."

"I know stuff about him, I know who he was," Doug tried to defend himself.

"I don't think she was well, even before she came here," I said.

"Sure she was, she was fine! Your dad was a bully! Pure and simple. Didn't she tell you?" Alison swung herself to face me again. I sat quiet, my head bowed. Then slowly I looked up and spoke to Alison.

"Mum never said much about my dad, except that he loved us but that we couldn't stay. She said that life here was too restrictive, she had to be a certain way and I would have to be that way too. She wanted me to have freedom and I would never have that here. She never said he bullied her or harmed her in any way, she never said she was afraid of him, but she did say that the house was dark and the trees would talk to her. The birds would watch her and when I asked her more she would tell me the stories – about the crows, about the king, about the island and the storms. She worked so hard to raise me and make me happy. I'm not a fool, I knew something had gone off between them, but it never mattered to me, just that she was safe. She was fine for months at a time and then something would set her off. She stopped explaining to people, they just sent her to the doctor and he'd give her pills. She's just sensitive to certain things, that's all, she doesn't need tablets, just to feel safe."

I turned to look at Doug, and put my hand over his and continued.

"Doug, she told me the stories, she told me the myths and legends. When she had an episode then it was the stories she believed, that the king was coming to get her, and me. She was really afraid. I think she was ill before she ever came here and it was just the life here that tipped her full into it."

"So why do you think she'd come here?" Doug asked quietly.

"Something happened at the house to frighten her, there were feathers and blood on the window, some wine and fruit trampled all over the floor. If she had an episode and nobody was there with her I think she might have been frightened enough to run away, right back here. She used to think he was coming to get me."

Doug squeezed my hand, "so she's run off like this before?"

"Never. We used to deal with it together. She would think he was coming to get her and I would be able to calm her down and explain that we were safe, tell her he couldn't cross water, like she'd taught me, and he couldn't touch us."

"What about the spells?" Asked Doug.

Alison shot a look at him and snapped, "What bloody spells? Have you gone mad?"

I smiled at her, "he could make spells to call us back, he would send birds to watch us, gifts to tempt us, he could lure us to the sea and draw us back across it with his powers. He could send envoys to trick us. Like poor Michael."

"You're as mad as he is, the pair of you, listen to yourselves. This is my friend Anna we're talking about here, who hitched up with a weirdo."

"My dad."

"Yeah, your dad, a man, pure and simple," Alison laughed and looked across at Doug.

"Just a man," I said, "but she didn't believe that, you knew how she was or you wouldn't have helped her."

119

"I've helped more than one girl get out of here, trust me. They meet some bloke, think it's true love and don't realise how they're expected to live. Cooped up at home, no money, a couple of kids for company, no real life. What about Lisa? Remember her Doug?"

Doug nodded, "Lisa was different, she was a clever girl and Yiannis was a dumb-ass fisherman with half a brain, who made a pile running his bar. He couldn't believe his luck when he landed her, and she thought she was going to live the simple life. He couldn't cope with how bright she was and used to hang out with bar girls, leave her at home with the baby, then come in nasty drunk. We got her on a flight to London. He thought she was going to the market with the kid. We'd sent some stuff ahead for her, a buggy, clothes, with a woman who'd been over on holiday. He didn't even know she was gone till late that night."

"It happens all the time, women just pack their bags, pick the kids up from school and jump on a plane with nothing more than a suitcase. Why d'you think the yiayias don't want their sons to marry foreigners? They're afraid they'll lose their grand-kids. Best to stick with the kind of man you understand, with ways you understand," she touched Doug's hand and dropped her head.

"My mum understood my dad, she said they were soulmates, loved each other, but he didn't know she was ill."

Alison stood up, "listen to me – there was nothing wrong with your mother when I first met her here. She was strong and clever and brave. It was him changed her, Korakas. We all thought he was a weirdo, none of the locals trusted him, half of them were afraid of him and he used that to make her afraid." She snorted a laugh, "Korakas! What kind of name is that? He wove mystery around him, to make him feel big. The crow! I ask you. He wove a web of lies around her, just as good as locking her in a cage. He stripped her of her friends, of everything that was about who she was and left her all alone with stories and threats out at that house. That's why I wanted her out of there, and you. It was him who made her ill, him who took your real mum away from you and left the one too scared to fight."

"That's true," whispered Doug, "when I first met your mom she had no fear, remember I told you how she stopped me taking the beating of my life, she spoke out, stuck up for everyone. He chose her because of her strength, and it is meeting him that changed the way she was."

I hesitated before speaking again, "I thought I saw her this morning you know, and Karen said she'd seen her here."
Alison rolled her eyes.

"Karen. She's been changed by this place too, and Doug. My lovely Doug, obsessed with island tales."

"Hey it's research baby, you know that. You'll be sorry when I write a book and make us a fortune."

"Where would Anna go if she came back here?"

"She'd come to us," said Alison, hesitantly.

"No, she'd find him." Doug seemed convinced

"That's what I think too," I said, "I think she would find him and ask him to leave us alone."

Then realising what Doug had said, I asked,

"What research?"

"Myths and shit, that's all."

"Yeah, shit is right," said Alison. "Shit that screwed up my best friend."

"Help me find her," I pleaded, reaching my hand up to Alison as she stood looking down at us both, "help me find her then, because I'm sure she's come back here."

"I've asked around. Nobody's seen her, or him and I can't even remember how to get to the house he used to have here in town."

"And we couldn't find the house in the hills, remember?" Doug paused, "just those ruins." Alison shot him a look of disbelief, her mouth opened, but Doug held up his hand to stop her.

"I went to a house with that guy, Xenon, it was up where you took me I'm sure."

"Who is that guy?" Doug seemed anxious.

"I've just seen him around," I felt defensive, "does it matter who he is?"

"It matters a great deal to us, you're our family," said Doug.

"He knows the island, he understands what I'm going through."

"What do you mean? What has he said? Where is he from?" Alison sat down again and stared at me.

"I don't know, alright. But he's been really kind and, he knows the place."

"Was that the guy in the truck?" Doug glanced at Alison as he spoke, "when I saw you I thought it was your dad for a moment."

"They all look the same to me," joked Alison.

"What did my dad look like?" Ally leaned forward.

"So tall," Doug held his hand in the air, "dark hair, dark eyes, nothing odd."

"Just a regular guy," said Alison.

"Look," said Doug. "We need to get this cleared up. The more I hear the more concerned I am."

"You're right," Alison sighed, "she'd never leave you like this, she swore she'd raise you strong and independent, but she would never disappear like this unless something was wrong."

"If you say she believed all the stories," said Doug, "maybe we should compare notes."

"Let's keep off the fairy stories, shall we? This is serious," Alison raised her voice.

"How about we all do what we do best," soothed Doug, "Al honey, you do the practical stuff. Ask around, check with the airport girls, see if she came in that way. Make up with Karen, see where she thinks she saw her, see if you can find out any hard news about her. What about Sylvie? Is she still around?"

"Who's she?" I asked.

"She used to work for Vassilis. Your mum worked for him too for a while. She lives out of town now. She knew a lot of people back then," said Alison. I caught Doug's eye before I spoke,

"I'll speak to Xenon, he seems to know what goes on here,"

"Keep away from that guy," snapped Doug.

"Doug, I'm just asking around, that's all."

"Doug's right," interrupted Alison, "keep strangers out of

this. Don't get involved with any men out here."

"For God's Sake! Lighten up will you," I could hear the words, but I had no control over what I was saying. They were right. I should look to them for help, my mother's oldest friends, nobody else. I was so angry that they felt threatened by Xenon. *He understands me.* As if he had heard my unspoken thoughts, Doug held my arm and said,

"Don't think you are the same as these people. You may think these stories are just that, but I'm telling you that this place has a past and the people are so tightly wrapped up in it that they don't live by the same rules you and I do. I'm telling you to be careful and respect that some of what I tell you is based in fact not fantasy." Doug was shaking, his neck reddened and the muscles tightened.

"Okay, I will. I'm sorry." I glanced across to Alison, who shook her head slowly.

"Just keep away from the men out here, they don't play the same game you do. Why don't you go and see Sylvie?"

"That'll keep me out of trouble will it?"

"Don't be like that," Alison soothed. "Sylvie's great, I've got a number somewhere, we could give her a call."

He is lying on the couch in the downstairs room, one arm across his eyes.

"I will never tire of you," *I whisper in his ear.*

It is almost dark outside, I have no idea of time, or the days of the week. The days are light and the nights dark, not like at home where we have to creep around in the dark on a winter morning. I don't ask where he's been, because he's back and that's all that matters. Although he watches me when he is here, I never feel trapped. It's when he's gone that I feel that.

Those birds in the trees watch me. One sits on the high wall, near the gate, as if daring me to leave. When they fly, they flap their huge wings effortlessly, beating the air, beat, beat, and travel twice as far as the small song birds who flap and dip across the sky in a flurry of activity.

"They are my envoys, my henchmen," *he tells me teasing.* "I am the King of the Ravens and they do my bidding. Beware, if you stray too far they will tell me and I will bring you back!" *Sometimes when he tells me these tales I look at him and see that his hair is as green-black as their plumage, it falls at the side of his face like wings on a bird. His nose is sharp and arched like a beak, his eyes are bright and dark, they switch here and there taking in every aspect of their view. I imagine him soaring above the town, watching the people below, then returning to me.*

" I will never tire of you," *I say again and stroke his face. It's lines and furrows give no clue to his age. He is dark, but not like the villagers. His hair is soft and falls in gentle layers against the side of his face. I have never seen him shave but his face is never more than lightly shadowed with dark hair.*

"How many years have you been on this island?" *I have spoken my thought out loud. He lets his arm fall away and opens* his eyes.

"Too many years, rai Anna, too many." He speaks in riddles, tells stories and legends, but never tells me who he is or where he came from.

"Why do you want to know about me? Why do you care who I am, where I am from?" He reads my thoughts again, "I know nothing about you, just that I was drawn to you because you can make me happy."

"Ask me then, I'll tell you about me." I am eager to tell him about my old life, although it seems irrelevant now. I can scarcely remember working, driving, shopping, my old friends.

"I have no need to know. You have no family, nobody you care to be with, or you would not be here with me."

I realise how true that is. With my mother's death I was released from all attachment to that old life, I am free to be wherever I choose. It's as if I have cut the ties and they never existed, except for the occasional reminder, a smell or a colour which brings my father or mother straight back into focus.

"I am your family now Anna." He wraps his arms around me and pulls me close to him. "And with our child, we shall be a new family."

It feels good when he talks like this. This is what my life should be, just us. I don't need anything from outside. He has this house, land and produce, some days he cooks for me, other days I cook for him. In the apothiki, a dark storeroom, is a huge barrel of wine, made from grapes from his vines and next to that tubs of olives from his groves.

"Tonight I will cook for you, no, I will take you out to eat. Go, get dressed."

As I climb into the pick-up, he throws a shawl around my shoulders. I don't need it, I'm wearing a jacket, but the smell comforts me, so I pull it up around my neck and bury my nose in the soft folds of the dark fabric. So much about him comforts me, the girl who was so restless. As we approach the harbour he turns right and follows the street to the waterfront. Most of the tavernas and bars have closed for the season, and the mood of the place is *very different from the height of the summer when I first came here. I can hear music as we park in the square by the waterfront, and hear the gentle slap of waves against the harbour wall and the hulls of the boats, the ting ting of ropes against a mast. Rhythmic. I can hear the rise and fall of the waves. He stands back to allow me to walk through the tables to one quite near the back. A waiter scurries forward, bowing his head to welcome us. The other customers watch as we pass and I feel like royalty. He pulls the chair out for me and settles me at the table before going inside to speak to the waiter again. The air I breathe has a hint of the sea, the slight odour of the fishing boats masked by the jasmine which grows across the wooden roof of the pergola where we sit. A giant ship's wheel sits to my left, surrounded by pots filled with foliage. A small boy is playing at being ship's captain.*

I feel a hand rest on my shoulder and look up to see he has come back and is watching the child play.

"We shall have a daughter."

"Not a son and heir?" I tease.

"I have no need of an heir. I will have a daughter as beautiful as her mother and as strong as her father."

My old self is embarrassed at how I let these moments pass without comment. When he speaks in that way of his, foretelling my future, organising my life, using such archaic language. My old self would have dealt him some clever quip. This new me accepts him. I wonder if this is who I really am? Perhaps here I'm settled because I'm allowed to defer to him, or a man like him, without defending my actions or lack of them. The waiter returns with a carafe of wine.

"From your vines," he nods to Korakas, as he pours some into my glass.

I am becoming accustomed to this wine. It's rich and full-bodied. It makes me light headed in a way I haven't felt with any other wine. Light-headed and yet I seem to be able to focus more on my surroundings. I become aware of the smells and sounds. If I close my eyes, I can feel him next to me. Once I have focussed on him, everything else falls back. I can smell him, hear his breath, feel the warmth of him. I stretch out my hand to touch his. I feel his long fingers, as they trace the shape of my face, run through my hair, follow the lines of my body, coaxing me, pulling at me, holding me. I open my eyes. Our fingers are just touching, his long and brown, mine stark white in comparison. The waiters bring platters of food. He feeds me with tasters from each and tells me their names, biriam.. bambes.. gigantes.. stacca.. koloukithea.. spinaki.. xtapothi.. ksifies. Strange words which make the food taste better. He watches me, smiles at me, holds my hand and then speaks.

"Come. We will take coffee." He wraps my arm through his as he leads me, not back to the pick-up but beyond the taverna into one of the small streets which runs away from the harbour, back towards the main town. We weave between bikes parked outside small houses until we come to a house in a side street. He leads me up the staircase to a door on the balcony. I remember this place. That day the boy died, I think we came here. He leads me into a small kitchen. Through the doorway to one side I can see a bed. He moves to the counter and reaches for the briki.

"No." I say. I can hear his breathing and mine. My head is light, but my thoughts are clear. I close my eyes, smell geranium, jasmine, coffee. I focus my thoughts. I smell him. I drop the shawl to the floor, move around the old wooden table between us, take the briki from him, placing it back on the counter. Every movement is considered.

"Come. I will make coffee - later." And for the first time, he lets me lead him. Into the bedroom.

The bus station was busy. A one-storey building stretched across one side of the yard, where buses were parked up displaying various destinations. I checked the piece of paper Alison had given me with the directions to the village where Sylvie lived now. None of the buses matched the name, so I dropped onto a bench to wait.

A handful of tourists waited to board a coach heading back to the major town in the East, where the main airport ferries tourists in and out of the island. An old woman sat herself down on the bench next to me. I pulled myself as far to the edge as I could to accommodate the expanse of the woman's behind. I lowered my face towards the scarf I wore across my shoulders and involuntarily breathed in. The familiar scent of washing powder filled my nostrils and I felt a pang of disappointment as I realised it no longer held that cold smell I had come to associate with Xenon.

That man kept disturbing my thoughts and creeping up on me when I least expected it. Since he had sat and watched me cry that day near the market, I felt as if he really did have some insight into the life I had been leading. If I questioned him he would never answer me directly, but sometimes he would mention an incident, or a place, a feeling, which revealed something about himself, or so I thought. Something about that man was familiar, as if we had known each other for a long time. Like I felt when I was with Pete, except with Pete there was no sexual tension at all. Hard as it was to admit it, with Xenon I found I had to fight to keep myself from giving in. The way he held himself, the way he spoke, the language he used, his confidence. If he laid his hand on me, the heat of him radiated through my clothes.

I understood why Alison acted so unimpressed, a woman like her would be of no interest to him whatsoever, and she was too old, older than mum, I thought. Alison was jealous. And Doug? Perhaps he was playing the paternal role, perhaps he knew his wife fancied the younger man and it made him mad. Perhaps Xenon was too like my father. Perhaps Alison had fancied Korakas and that was why she was so bitter about him. Maybe she had been jealous of my mother and that was why she helped to split them up.

"Perhaps you would prefer a lift." I felt a hand on my shoulder and turned, knowing that it was Xenon before I saw him.

"Where are you going?" He asked. As he leaned forward his shirt fell open slightly. Around his neck was a fine cord and on it swung a ring, or rather half a ring. It was honey coloured gold, regular on one side, but waved as if cut about its circumference, to make another ring. My hand flew to my chest where my own silver ring rested against my skin.

"I was coming to find you," I replied.

"So why wait here for a bus? If you want me, just call me and I shall appear." He was laughing at me again. A man shouted from across the yard and Xenon looked across to him. Running his hand from my shoulder down my arm, he leant forward and whispered, "I must go, but I will find you this evening."

He disappeared through the crowd of tourists and I couldn't work out which way he had gone. A horn sounded and a bus pulled in, bearing the name of the village I was supposed to be visiting. Meeting this woman Sylvie seemed unimportant now. I touched the ring around my neck and closed my fingers tightly round it. The large woman next to me waddled over to the bus and pulled herself up the steps. I followed. Stick to your plans.

The bus took the main road to the east, dropping some passengers off at the side of the highway. It dropped off the main road to divert to villages where others stepped off. I concentrated hard on the place names. Doug had been specific about where I should get off. At last I saw the large hotel he had told me to look out for, and counted the number of junctions until the village sign came into view. He had told me not to get down at the first sign, but the second. From the bus stop I was to walk down the track towards the village. Not so much a track though. The junction with

129

the main road was well defined and signposted. It must be several years since Doug and Alison had been this way. The village they described was still visible, taverna names they had mentioned, but newly built apartments lined the road, bars and shops filling in the spaces which must have been empty years before. Street lights lined the road and a few metres down there were pavements.

I reached the square and checked Doug's notes for the name of the bar where I was to meet Sylvie. At a far table sat a woman in a floral kaftan and a floppy black hat. I stopped in front of her and the woman looked me up and down, before cocking her head to one side.

"Anna's daughter, right?" Her accent was American, but softer than Doug's, with a lilt to it, as if English were no longer her primary tongue and she had adopted the local one instead.

"Yes," I replied simply, "how did you know?"

"The way you walk, your eyes, your skin." I shifted the weight from one foot to the other, aware that I was being studied.

"I wondered,"

"Yeah?" The woman smiled.

"Do you still work for the travel company?"

"Not now, no."

"Oh," I hesitated.

"Is that what you were wondering?" The woman teased.

"My mother has gone missing and I thought she might have come here, the island I mean."

"Missing?"

"I know it sounds ridiculous, but my mum's always been kind of,"

"I know about your mom, how she is I mean. And Doug and Al told me why you're here. How do you think I can help?"

"If she came back, her name would be on a passenger list. I thought you could check."

"I see," Sylvie gestured to me to sit down and pulled her chair closer to the table, she rested her arms across it and clasped her hands together.

"If she flew in from the UK I can ask one of the reps to

130

check the lists, you know, the company lists. They aren't supposed to obviously, but you know, they've known me for years. If she flew in from the mainland it might be trickier, but I'll try. Of course she's more likely to have come in to the other airport, more flights in that way. If she came by boat that would be harder. I know a girl married to a ferry captain, maybe he could check, I don't know."

I grasped the woman's hands, "Thank you so much," I felt my throat tighten.

"Hey," Sylvie put her hand to my cheek. "I'd do anything to help Anna and you. I was so happy she managed to leave. And look at you, all grown up and so beautiful. It was the right thing to do." She looked into my eyes and lowered her voice.

"I tried to go once."

I looked straight back at her, "why?"

"Oh my husband drank, we fought a lot, you know, stuff like that," she stopped, uncertain, but then continued. "My boss arranged it, booked the flights to the UK for me and my son. I left for work as usual, yiayia took my son to play-school. I stopped off at the office, picked up the tickets, a hire car, called in at the play-school, collected my son at lunch time, said he had a dental appointment. We drove to the airport, just like a regular working day, no luggage, we checked in, everyone thought I was working, checking in clients, meeting new arrivals, then we got on the plane. From the UK we took flights to the US." Sylvie looked past me and stopped talking.

"But you came back," I prompted.

"I had no money, no job. Welfare is not a good way to live. It's not like welfare in England. I'd left home at eighteen, I had no trade, no qualifications, just gone travelling and ended up here. I was earning good money here. We struggled along, but my husband came to find me. He begged me to come back with him, said he'd change. So I came back."

"My dad never followed us."

"Your dad was different."

"That's what you all say," I paused. "Did your husband change?"

"Well, he kept the passports pretty close for a while. I had

131

another child. This is their home."

"Did you want to stay?"

"Life is different these past few years. When I met your mom we didn't have phones at the house, now we've got it all, phones, mobiles, the web. We're not so isolated."

"My mum said I would have no choices if we'd stayed here."

"Like I say, it's different now and your dad was different. He wielded such control."

"Thank you," I sighed.

"For what?"

"You make it all seem so normal. Doug and Alison and Karen, they make it seem so crazy. I've been in a real state."

"Doug and Alison have always fought about who your dad was, Doug with his mad stories. Some people can live here and some cannot. Anna was changed by it, she needed to get away. She needed to take you away and like I say, the right choice."

"If she came back here, where would she go?"

"People always come back. Just to look. But it's never the same. I reckon she'd look up Doug and Alison. If she hasn't done that then I don't know, maybe she's not here at all. Why not contact the consulate?"

"It seems a little crazy, like I'm over-reacting."

"And you don't think that traipsing round like a headless chicken isn't a little crazy? Go home, Ally. See the island and go home."

I shivered and readjusted my scarf around my shoulders, comforted by its scent, then realised that it had smelled differently an hour before. I looked around to see if Xenon were anywhere close by.

"What's up?" Sylvie looked alarmed.

"I just thought, just felt chilled. Stupid." I stood up to leave, then added, "Sometimes I feel like I'm being watched. I met this man..."

Sylvie grasped my hand and whispered, "Don't get close to anyone here. Be careful. Go home and forget all this stuff." Then she threw her head back and laughed aloud, as if for an audience, raised her voice and continued, "Bye then honey. Safe trip. Send me a postcard," and pushed me away from her.

I began the walk back towards the bus stop, my hand involuntarily reaching for the ring at my neck. As I reached the edge of the square I turned to look back, and saw a man holding Sylvie by the elbow. Her head was bowed and the man was leaning in to her, shaking his head as he spoke. Sylvie wiped her hand across her eyes and the man released her. As I watched, the man looked up and straight at me. His features were sharp, his dark hair fell across his face as he turned again, for a moment I thought... but then he guided Sylvie out of sight.

We are driving up to the mountains today. The caps have been covered with new snow for a week now.

"Keep warm today, wear this." He throws me the green-black shawl and I wrap it around me under the big coat he found for me. My summer clothes seem ridiculous now. I wish I had some of my things from back – home – I was going to say, but this is home and that is England. My whole past lies in three old suitcases and a few boxes in the garage of a work colleague from back then. I wish I had my boots. Again, as if reading my mind, he pulls open the cupboard door and takes out a pair of long black leather boots, the kind the old men wear in the villages. I pull them on, up, under my jeans.

"We will eat in the mountains. You must eat. I think perhaps you eat too little."

One thing mars our time together, each month regular as clockwork. Each time anger and disappointment are side by side in his face. I feel I'm letting him down, that it's my fault.

The road is unusually busy, many of the locals are driving up to see the snow. We wind our way up, taking each bend closely, until we reach a village on the edge of a plain. The road signs are littered with bullet holes here, target practice for the local boys. We stop for a meze before heading further up the track, where we find drifts of snow. All around us people are rolling snow into balls and lifting these onto the bonnets of their cars. We follow suit and drive back down the mountain to the town. I am laughing, because I feel part of a community again. All of us trying to transport snow back down the mountain to show our friends in the harbour.

In the kafeneon I can see some of the old crowd. We park the truck a short distance away and walk arm in arm to the group. Alison jumps up and rushes to hug me.

"Oh we've missed you," she almost shouts. Then, whispered in my ear, "are you okay?"

"Yes, I'm fine. More than fine." He follows behind me and makes a great show of shaking hands with them all, ordering food and beers. He watches, as I sit and talk, smiling at me, but watching. He peels large prawns from the meze and passes me one, then throws the shell to floor. A big black bird swoops down effortlessly and hops towards it, grabbing it in its beak before flying off again with that slow beat of its wings. I want them to know that I am happy, but I feel like I have to justify myself, I am apologising, making excuses. I want to tell them that I love him, but I seem unable to say the words.

"We're trying for a baby," I say instead. It seems foolish and yet I seem so certain when I am with him.

"And this was whose idea?" says Alison.

"Anna!" He calls me softly, but firmly. "We must go now. Look our man is melting." I look at the truck to see the huge ball of snow is slowly melting away to nothing, a lump of ice, precariously lodged on the bonnet. I kiss the girls, wave and follow him. He seems unhappy and I'm afraid I've upset him.

The room was dark. I lay on the bed, a sheet draped across me. A motorbike whined past and a man called out into the night. The air lay on my skin and pressed on the sheet until it felt like a lead weight, I kicked it off and looked down at myself. White skin with a fine tracery where a strap had lain, or a skirt stopped short of my knees, shades of light skin. I tried to imagine what my mother had been like when she had first come to the island. In her paintings she depicted herself as a white figure against a dark backdrop. Every summer I laboured to get a good sun tan and mum always laughed at my efforts. You'll get used to being pale and interesting. Perhaps Sylvie was right, I should see the island, where I was born, and go home and wait for my mother to come back. Here on the island I was confused. I felt drugged, my thoughts were not my own. That man Xenon seemed to know what I was thinking before I did, Doug and Alison were too busy arguing between themselves and Sylvie had been no help at all. A shaft of light from the street light outside fell across my body and the ring I wore on the chain around my neck, glinted. Lots of people wore something round their neck, so it wasn't particularly strange that Xenon had a ring around his and yet I knew as much as I denied the similarity, that the ring he wore was like the one mum and I had. My head ached. I found it hard to sleep at night, the heat made it difficult, or the sounds outside, or the buzzing of mosquitoes. Just a few hours until dawn.

I sat up and swung my legs over the side of the bed. I saw the briki on the stove and decided to make myself a coffee. The familiar task brought a memory of my mother. For the first time I felt afraid that I may never stand next to her, or touch her, that memory may be all I had left. As if the grieving process had already begun, I sniffed as I stirred the coffee over the heat. Don't break the waves. Too late. The coffee boiled up and over the top of the pan and the unmistakable smell of burned coffee filled the small room.

Pulling on a pair of jeans and a shirt and stuffing my scarf into my bag, I left the room and walked down to the harbourfront. The night sky was growing lighter by the minute. I saw a group of girls wandering arm in arm, on the way home from a night out. A man drove past on a Vespa, the unmistakeable sound of the engine putt-putting into the distance. I glanced over my shoulder, aware that I should be careful so early in the morning, but I felt exhilarated, nobody knew where I was, nobody could call on a mobile. I was free, for the first time in my life. I followed the curve of harbour until I came to Costa's café and sat at one of the tables near the front. The memory of my mother was becoming harder to capture, I was losing the sense of her. I was losing the will to find her. *She's gone. Give it up.*

I'm alone again in the house. He left early this morning and no word of when he'll be back. It's cold. There's a wood burner in the main room, but I can't get it going. The air is damp, even inside the house. I'm flicking through the few channels we have on the old TV. Nothing. Unless you count re-runs of American soaps, or those creepy shadow puppet shows or CNN. I sort through my few belongings and realise how little of me is left. I wander into the kitchen and begin to make coffee, the ritual I have learned from him. Just as it reaches the point where I should pull it off the heat, I hear those damn birds outside and look up from what I'm doing to see what's disturbed them.

"Rai Anna, you've broken the waves," *he is beside me.*

"I didn't hear you come in." *I feel nervous, guilty, as if he's caught me out in some way. He strokes my hair.*

"You are lonely."

"Sometimes, yes."

"I neglect you. My Anna, who I chose from all the others." *He sighs and walks out into the courtyard, down the steps to the store where he keeps the wood. He runs back up the stairs two at a time, with his arms full of wood, and drops it by the wood burner. Within minutes he has a good fire going and settles me in front of it. He throws one of the soft dark rugs around my shoulders and fusses as he settles me on the couch.* "I will take better care of you."

"I couldn't get the fire going. It's so cold in the winter and wet."

"Never as wet as when the storms come. An island like this one needs to be purged. These people take it for granted, they drift through the summer," *he snapped twigs for kindling as he spoke and threw them in the basket at the side of the stove.*

"They work hard in the summer." *I've seen how hard is to*

get through a season here. They make their money in the summer to provide for the winter, seven days a week, into the early hours of each morning.

"So they work hard. But they whine and complain. The winter reminds them to be grateful for the months of plenty." His face twitches as he speaks. His mood changed again. I could kick myself for being so stupid. I should know not to contradict, unless I really need to. What does it matter whether the people work hard or not? What matters is that we're happy. I try to bring him back to me. I pull him to me on the couch, wrap my arms around him, press against him. I breathe in that sharp, clean smell he has. I wish I could clothe myself in it, then we would be the same and he would believe that I didn't want to be anywhere else, or be with anybody else.

"Let me cook for you tonight, let me spoil you." I try and make my voice as soft as the covers he wraps me in, to coax him back to how he was a moment ago. But I'm rarely able to do this. He will change when he's ready. He pushes me off him and stands up.

"I will show you how these people are reminded of their place in the order of things." He marches out of the room and returns wearing his heavy jacket, my coat thrown over his arm. "Come."

He holds the coat out for me and helps me into it, tucking me into it like his child. We leave the house and he opens the door of the pick-up for me. It's raining. It's been raining for days now. He begins to talk as we drive up the track towards the main road. He seems upset. His eyes glisten, with tears? I'm not sure. He's angry and when he's angry he frightens me, but I love his passion. When he's angry I know he feels like an outsider, just like me.

"You say they work hard? These village idiots? They are driven by greed. They renege on promises, they lie to achieve their version of success and they lose what is truly good through their own stupidity. And my father too, and my mother, they fell for this place and were changed by it. Lost what they had. These people will never come to anything, they are nothing more than children. They will never have control of this place. It is wasted on them." He spits the words. I can do nothing but sit quietly while he continues his

139

rant. He throws the pick-up around the bends as we weave down the hillside to the main road. The windscreen wipers flick back and forth, angrily swiping the rain from the screen, in sympathy with him. He stops. He stops the truck and he stops speaking. The rain falls and the wipers carry on sweeping the windscreen, giving me a momentary glimpse of the track ahead.

"Your father and mother?" I ask because I need to know who he is and what he comes from. I ask quietly because I'm afraid I'll set him off again. He looks at me surprised, as if he had forgotten I was there.

"Anna." Calm again. "Anna. They make me crazy, these people. This island makes me crazy sometimes. If I could take you away, we could be happy I'm sure. You give me strength, but more than that, I know you love me." He turns to face the road again and moves off. We join the main road and drive for a few hundred metres before turning off towards the town.

I'm still afraid. I can never predict how he'll react. He says he knows I love him. That must make him feel good. I do love him. He seems so alone up there at the house and I know he needs me. When he lies in my arms his face softens and he looks so young. When I hold him at night I have a real purpose. I know my role. I ache physically to have a child for him, because that will make him happy. If we had a child he'd know for sure I'd never leave him.

He parks up on the pavement some way from the sea front and we walk towards the harbour. I can hear the waves before I see them. The sea has risen until it is level with the street. Debris litters our way. Concrete planters from outside tavernas, have been knocked sideways with the power of the waves. As we approach the front, a huge wave rises up over the harbour front, crashes across some chairs left outside a café and drags them back in the sea. A girl who had been walking slightly ahead of us hesitates as she sees this and then, pulling her coat to her begins to walk ahead again, past the shops and bars. He runs after her and drags her back, close to where I am standing. He is shouting at her and she is pointing across the harbour to a bar on the far side. I can't hear because the sound of the wind and the waves is drowning out any other sounds.

He shakes her by the arm until she gives in and walks back the way we have just come, disappearing behind a café up an alleyway that runs parallel to the sea, behind the houses.

"You see how crazy they are? She works at the bar on the far side. She thinks she can walk round while this is going on," he jerks his head at the waves which are a thrashing brown mass. We walk behind our usual kafeneon and climb the steps to a bar which overlooks the harbour. It has a balcony which runs along the front of the property. In the summer you can sit outside and watch the tourist's antics below. Today we sit at the bar and gaze out of the window at the sea's antics. In the distance I make out the bent figure of the girl, who has reached the other side via the back street. She hesitates, gauging the rise and fall of the sea, before she runs the last few metres to the bar where she works.

Alex, the owner, greets us warmly, waving the bartender aside as she stretches towards the bottle of cheap schnapps they offer to customers as a welcome.

"No. Anna drinks what I drink." He bows his head in that way they have. The door is flung open and a young local rushes in laughing. He rattles off a story, making the men laugh. I hear the name Babis several times. Alex explains, for my benefit.

"Babis has lost his truck! That crazy boy thought he could race the sea and tried to drive to the harbour from the west. His new truck you know? It's big, four by four. New, I tell you. A wave comes over the top and the truck stops. He tries to start it, his baby truck, you know? His friend, he's making a show for his friend of course! His friend says, 'Babis moray! Get out of the truck!' But Babis won't listen, he tries and tries the engine. Another wave comes, his friend jumps out. The truck moves, but not by the engine, you understand? And Babis, finally he jumps. And what happens to his beautiful truck? The waves take it, straight into the sea!"

"You see," says Korakas, in my ear, "stupid people." He walks away to speak to some men in the corner of the bar, smiling at me as he goes. Alex leans forward and whispers to me.

"You see this," and he gestures through the window to the scene below. "This is what happens when the summer has gone and we have taken our fill of all it has to offer. We cannot take what we enjoy and not suffer some consequence. When you live on an island such as this, you must understand the ways. Katalaves? You understand?"

I smile at him and sip my drink. They love the sound of their own voices this lot. "And your friend," he nods towards Korakas, "know that he is at one with this island. Many women have tried to be where you are now, but he chose you. He will protect you, but see what he can do and beware." He sweeps his hand again to take in the scene below in the harbour. The rain is lashing against the window and I see the reflection of Korakas in it, standing next to me.

"What is he saying? What stories does he tell now?"
Alex laughs and raises his glass, "I am telling the beautiful Anna how she must dedicate her life to her master and make him happy for all our sakes!" He downs the drink in one and bowing, walks away. He seems unafraid of Korakas. Most men defer to him in some way, even Nikos all that time ago in the harbour, when they had the row about Jan. But Alex seems to walk with confidence and meet him as an equal.

"He doesn't make you angry?" I ask him.

"Alex? He has been a friend for many years, a faithful friend. He likes to tell stories, but every time it is a different one. You must be careful what you believe when he speaks."

One by one café owners arrived to open up their shops for the day's business. Costas and his brother arrived and nodded at me as I sat watching their morning routine. Costas unlocked the door and went inside for a moment before reappearing with a hose, and proceeded to clean down the street outside his café, leaning under tables, pushing dust and discarded cigarettes, small pieces of food dropped under foot until they reached a gulley and ran into the sea over the edge of the harbour wall. He playfully squirted a big black bird which hopped across the rivulet of dirty water, pecking for morsels. He laughed and said something to me which I didn't understand, but I smiled anyway. He called out to his brother and the flow of water stopped.

"Kafe?"

"Nai," I answered, "parakalo," I smiled again, pleased with our simple exchange. Here in the café, I felt at peace, no questions to answer, no demands being made. Costas returned with a steaming cup of coffee, I sipped it slowly, enjoying the sensation of the heat on my face. Life continued here, as if nothing were out of place. If I relaxed I could forget everything and yet every sip of coffee or mouthful of food seemed like a betrayal, an acceptance that mum was gone from me. I lifted my hand to my chest where the ring lay under my t-shirt. I wrapped my fingers around it, through the cloth. Gesturing to Costas that I would be back, I walked the few hundred yards to the kiosk on the corner and pulled my phone card from my bag. I hesitated , then allowed my fingers to dial the number, prompting my memory. I listened to the ring tone, an echo of that old life in England.

A voice answered with the name of the restaurant. I could hear sounds of the bar in the background, voices, laughter, 'bottling up,' remembering the familiar morning routine, a world away.

"Richard?" My voice was strained,

"Sorry, no, can I take a message?" A clear English voice, unfamiliar, no lilt or strain of accent. I felt so far away from them all now. I was silent.

"Ally? Is that you? Ally?"

I held the receiver close to my ear and imagined the restaurant, matched the sounds to the memories. Then another voice, "Ally? Is that you?"

"Richard," I was relieved.

"Ally, where are you?"

"On the island."

"The island?"

"I need to find mum."

"To find her? But Ally," his voiced softened, "are you on your own?"

"No. I met some of mum's old friends. Richard?"

"Yes love?"

"About mum," I couldn't finish the sentence.

"Ally, tell me where you are, let me come and fetch you." Silence. "Ally?"

As I replaced the receiver it was as if Richard, the restaurant and that whole life back there, ceased to exist. I felt that pleasant sensation of my skin tightening under the heat of the sun. I allowed the sounds around me to creep back in to my consciousness. Walking back towards the kafeneon I watched Costas as he wiped down tables, ready for the morning crowd. He waved as I approached and pointed to a fresh cup of coffee on the table where I had been sitting. As I sipped it I battled with the over-riding feeling that I was alone, and my mother was gone.

This morning I fling the windows wide open. Winter has gone and only the white caps of the mountains betray the fact that it was ever here at all. Korakas was up early and left before I got out of bed. I creep back under the covers and pull them up around me, just to smell him. I can hear the sound of the chickens, a dog in the distance, those birds in the trees. I close my eyes and breathe. I imagine him coming back to me, cold to the touch. He lies on top of me and presses close to me and rubs his face into my neck. If I could stay just here, with him, in this bed, we would be fine. No rows, no stories, no doubts.

Something has disturbed those birds. They have a way of calling, as if giving off an alarm. The dog barks a way off again, then a disgruntled clucking from the chickens, as if they have been interrupted from an important task, rather than pecking and scratching. I listen hard and hear the sound of a motorbike. I know the engine. I know them all. Alison and I used to sit outside her restaurant and guess who was coming just by the sound the engine made as it rounded the corner. And this is a throbbing sound, throaty, then a tick, tick, tick as the chain rattles, the bike slowing to come through the gates. Doug. It must be Doug. I pull on a pair of jeans and a jumper from the heap on the chair and run out to see.

"I knew it was you!" I'm surprised at how pleased I am to see him. I've just been lying in bed wishing it was just the two of us and yet a second later I am relieved that someone is here. I fling myself at him and hold him tight.

"Hold on." He pushes me gently away to take a look and can see I am crying. "What's up? Why the tears?"

"I don't know." I really don't know. I take him by the hand and into the house. He watches while I make coffee.

"I love to watch you make coffee. Al makes instant shit."

"Ah, if you were mine, I'd make you coffee all day long."
I love to tease him. Then I feel ashamed. What if Korakas heard
me talking like this? I have pulled clothes on over my naked body
and now I am standing in the kitchen making coffee, laughing and
teasing as if this man is my lover. I glance out of the window just as
one of those black birds spreads its wings and flies off over the trees.

"Anna? You okay?"

"I'm fine." I hand him his coffee and tell him I'm going to
get dressed.

"Hey relax, only me." He chats so easily. I have forgotten
what English sounds like from a native speaker. The contrast
between him and Korakas seems so stark. I have no need to choose
the words before I speak, Doug understands every phrase, attempt
at humour, ironic statement. With Korakas I have to be so careful. I
hurt him sometimes because he doesn't understand what I mean. I
find myself talking less and less and listening to him, just responding
to what he asks.

"So how is he? Are you happy?"

"So happy. He makes me feel small and protected. He loves
me."

"And you? Do you love him?"

"Yes I do." I am embarrassed to talk of love. He needs
me and that feels good. He seems to think of me as some kind of
precious thing, which is why he gets angry when I disappoint him.
I struggle to know what love is. It seems to involve possession and I
fight against being a possession. I need to feel free.

"Just wish we saw more of you hon, that's all. We miss you."
And I miss them all terribly, but I can't tell Doug that. He'll want to
know what's keeping me away.

"Why don't you come down to the harbour any more?"
If I ask to go down, he thinks I don't want to be with him. If nobody
else existed that would be fine. Me and him. I would be happy.

"I've been quite busy." I hear myself say.

"Yeah? Just so long as you're happy."

TAKE ME WITH YOU

"More than."

146

TAKE ME AWAY

"I hadn't realised what I wanted out of life Doug. You rush around, you work, go out. What's it for? Up here we have each other."

BEFORE HE COMES BACK

"I'm at peace. And if only we could have a child we'd be a family. Look at this place. It's beautiful. I have everything, a home, good food, clean air, a man who would kill for me." I try and drown out that other voice in my head.

YES HE WOULD

Doug sits me down at the table and pushes my coffee over to me.

"Drink it." He says. "We're all looking for a connection with someone special Anna, look at me and Al. It's great. But we need outside stuff too, to keep alive. I believe this guy wants you, I've seen the way he looks at you. But he's not like the rest of us and you know it. Me and Al have a tough enough time of it, she's so damn English and I know she thinks I'm a dumb-ass American. He doesn't think the same as you, talk the same as you. You don't know anything about him. I'm not playing dad here, I'm just saying that we love you too and we want you to be safe and happy."

The voice in my head has stopped. Doug's little speech has drowned it out. "Doug. I'm fine. I love my time up here. The harbour doesn't stimulate me. All idle chat and drinking, the tourists in the summer and the pickers and drop-outs in the winter. That's not for me. You have your flying buddies to keep you busy and Alison. Be happy that I've found someone for me."

I watch as he rides off again, listen as the sound of his bike gets further away. The chickens have settled and the black birds are back in the trees, quiet now. I wander back into the kitchen to clear the cups away. I feel a moment of panic.

A busy street on a Saturday, I have let go of my father's hand
for a moment to look in a shop window. I take his hand again
and look up to see a stranger, same coat and dark trousers,
but the wrong man. Panic. But then I see my real dad and run
to take his hand. I am safe again.

"So who was here?" I hadn't heard the truck.

"Oh. Doug, you know Doug and Alison." The inference being they both came.

"Two cups?"

He rocks one of the cups on the draining board.

"She only drinks that instant shit," it trips off my tongue. No lies.

"Come here." He pulls me close and slips his hands under my jumper to feel my skin.

"You had a man here, dressed like this?"

"Doug's not a man, he's Alison's Doug."

How will this go? Will he laugh? How was his day? Will he turn and leave? Will he shout?

"Let me show you how I'd dress for you." I slip away from his grasp, unzip my jeans and let them drop to the floor.

"I missed you this morning," I whisper.

He folds his great arms around me and I know I'm safe again.

Across the harbour I could see the other café owners busying themselves with deliveries, one by one the shops and stalls opened for the day. Unsure of my next move, I slipped some money under my coffee cup and headed away from the harbour and towards the main town. At the top of the street lined with tourist shops, past the church, I crossed a tree-lined square. Here taxi drivers waited for their next fare, drinking coffee, playing Tavli, I passed a cake shop, pausing for a while to look at the confections in the window, remembering my mother's description of a sickly sweet milk pudding. *She has walked these streets*, I thought, *seen these trees, these buildings.* Beyond the square was a long, low city building, tatty green paint-work. I made out some of the letters BIBLIO and guessed this might be a library. I remembered Doug had said something about working there to keep out of Alison's way. I had a sudden idea that I could discover some of the island's folklore myself without dragging him into it.

A smiling girl, about my age, greeted me at the desk. In that disarming way the locals have of gauging a person's nationality, she launched straight into English.

"Hello, your first visit to our library, yes?"
I faltered before answering, "yes, do you have any books about your island history, in English?"

"Ah, very little I am sorry to say, but please, let me show you what we have." She stood back to let me pass, "we are unable to allow you to remove the books of course, unless you are able to provide your residency to me of course, your home that is."

"That's fine, I'd just like to look."

The girl showed me into a room with long tables between shelving. She directed me to the old wooden filing drawers and explained which held the cards for English language books and how the cataloguing system worked.

"We are of course intending a computer system to begin, but this is our old library. We have some very old books, very beautiful, but I am sorry to say they are not in English." She gestured towards some shelves at the back of the room containing large leather bound volumes.

"I leave you now." Still smiling, she disappeared towards her desk at the far end of the room.

The warm weather has thawed him. Just like the mountains, he has shrugged off the winter. His face is light, he smiles softly as he watches. He still watches me, but I feel warmth when he does. And today I sit at the wheel of my own car. Well, an old car, not in my name, but a car for me to drive. One of the English left it here, didn't think it would make the trip back home when they left. It happens, they leave and sell everything they have accumulated. Funny, the ones who intend to pass through, stay, and the ones who arrive with their entire lives in tow rarely last more than one winter. What is it that keeps us here and drives those others away? He leans through the car window, "here," he pushes some money into my hand, "drive carefully," and kisses me on the cheek, like my father, not my lover. I am exhilarated as I weave down the mountainside, hugging the edge of the road, coasting, window down, air streaming through, a little cold, the sun not yet high, not yet hot. He has given me my freedom. Somehow I have earned this.

I reach the town without recalling the route I take. The old men are gathered in the square, talking to the taxi drivers who sit waiting for fares. I turn down the approach to the harbour and realise the chain has been slung across the street at the bottom. The new season has begun. I turn the car to the right and drive around the back of the harbour to find a space to park. The harbour has a buzz, waiters set up tables outside, the beer man trundles past with a trolley load of crates. There is an air of expectancy, the start of something new. I break into a run as I see Alison walking ahead, arm in arm with Doug. Calling to them as I run. Doug stops and turns when he hears my voice, but Alison hesitates before following him. He walks towards me his arms open to greet me.

"Hey hon. How the devil are you?" His smile wraps round me before his arms do the same. He squeezes the breath out of me.

"Good to see you, isn't it?" He turns to ask Al.

"Yeah, it is," and at last she comes forward to kiss me, first on one cheek then the next.

"Where's his highness?" She links her arm through mine and we walk on round the harbour.

"Surveying his kingdom," I decide to humour her. Nothing can spoil the way I feel today. A boy walks out of a café and empties the contents of a bucket across our path. Steaming, black water flows across the paving slabs towards the edge of the harbour wall and drips down into the water below. Alison jumps over in one stride but Doug and I tiptoe through pulling faces. A black bird hops across to inspect the puddle, pecking through the rivulets.

"I hate those birds." Alison and Doug both look at me and I realise I have spoken out loud, so I laugh, "they're like rats, always on the scavenge."

"Yiasou Anna!" Costas from the kafeneon calls out. He is beaming at me and waving a bottle of beer in the air, "Ela," he beckons us inside. He fusses around us, pulling two tables together, dusting down the chairs and brings us a couple of beers which he divides between four glasses.

"Stin iyia sas!" He raises his glass to me and we all drink, calling 'yiamas' in reply.

"Ali-son," he speaks her name awkwardly, "when you open restaurant?"

"Probably next week." She turns to me, "fancy a job?"

"I might do."

"Really?"

"Yeah, why not?"

"Thought you wouldn't be allowed." Doug laughs uneasily and shoots a look between the two of us, but I let it pass.

The catalogues of English language books were uninspiring. I drifted towards the book shelves and leafed through volumes wondering at the words written on the page. I had never mastered the art of matching the symbols to the sounds and felt foolish now. A girl born here who couldn't decipher the language beyond the basics. I turned to the larger volumes at the back of the room, some of these contained drawings and plans of cities, maps and charts. Here was a simple map of the island, I recognised the shape. Some script and then a sketch of a labyrinth, a man, Minos I thought, wearing some kind of headdress. Turning the pages I tried to reassemble all the memories of stories told to me from childhood, at school, by my mother, filtered down through television and film. The Labyrinth, the Minotaur, here was Icarus falling from the sky. Then I turned the page to see my mother's face looking back at me, the shape of her lips, the slant of her eyes, a tear poised to fall, anguish showing in every line across her forehead, around her eyes. I slammed the book shut. A man sitting quietly at one of the tables glared at me. "I'm sorry," I whispered, and then, "do you speak English?" The man shook his head in annoyance.

"Please, can I help?" The girl had returned. She glanced at the volume I had been reading and smiled. "Ah, this is a special book, very beautiful images, stories and mythologies."

"There is a picture, of a woman, do you know who she is?" I tried to find the picture, my hand shaking as I turned the pages.

"There are many stories about the island and about the people who have lived here," the girl explained, "some are in this book. You see," she halted my hand at an image of Icarus, "this of course is Icarus, son of Daedalus. Daedalus they say was a great inventor, some say a thief and a murderer. He came to our island in shame, having killed a young student who he feared was more clever than he. This boy had invented a simple saw, inspired by the bone of a fish or some say from watching the jaws of an ant. But Daedalus took the invention for his own. But of course you know the story."

"Some of it, I know about the labyrinth and Icarus burning his wings."

"Ah yes, the wings. Some historians believe that the wings were in fact sails of a boat, that Daedalus simply crafted sails for small boats. Unheard of by Minos, whose ships were powered by the paddle, or rather oars, I believe is the word. Icarus and his father had wings in this way, for their boats to fly away. A more modern explanation I think, than the actual wings of wax and feather. My preferred explanation of events."

I turned the pages again and stopped at the image of the woman.

"Who is this?" I could hardly speak the words, my chest felt tight.

"Ah! You are very like this lady!" She seemed delighted, leant forward and held her finger on the page, reading the words beneath. "An ancient script, forgive me," she paused and then read, "Minos had many slaves, none more beautiful than Naucrate."

"And this is Naucrate?"

"Shall I read it to you?"

"Please."

"Of course, but first excuse me I will inform my colleague, she may need me at some point."

"Oh, if it's a problem," I gushed, inwardly begging the girl to get on with it and just read.

"No problem." I gazed at the picture until the girl returned and gestured to me to take a seat at the table next to her. Faltering to start, but gaining in confidence as she translated, the girl began to read me the story.

"Minos had many slaves, none more beautiful than Naucrate. Not only was she beautiful to gaze upon, but she would sing for him and talk to him of her own land and her own people, their customs

154

and their desires, how they lived and how they worshipped, what they believed in and what they dreamed of. And as much as any King can love a slave, he loved Naucrate."

"And the picture," I interrupted, " that's Naucrate?"

"Yes, I think so." The girl continued. "Daedalus came to hear of this girl who walked with the king and talked to him as if she too had royal blood. He wished to learn more of her power over the king, so he fashioned a great bird and placed it in a tree. From afar he could watch her, as if he himself was there looking down at her, for just as the moon reflects the light of the sun, so the bird's polished eyes reflected what it saw below and Daedalus looked on from his vantage point. As Naucrate walked amongst the lemon trees, Daedalus vowed to have her for his own. And knowing that his works pleased Minos greatly, he demanded that his reward should be this girl.

King Minos, believing that Daedalus was a loyal follower, capable of building a great civilisation for him, and desiring to keep the favour of this man, granted him a meeting with Naucrate. But first he spoke to Daedalus.

This is no ordinary slave. This is Naucrate from a far off land. She is a gift, a woman of extraordinary power of spirit, she has the inner strength of any man, and an intellect to equal your own. I cannot give her to you, for although by my law she is a slave, I am unable to command her heart and without her heart she is nothing. You must win her love and if she desires, I will grant her permission to be with you. But I tell you this, you may marvel in how softly she treads, at her gentle voice, her pale skin, the shape and colour of her eyes, which are as the almonds from my finest trees, the way her lashes fall against her cheek which flushes when she speaks, but this young woman is as old as my island and she bears ancient wisdom which must be respected. Any man who believes he can be her master will suffer.

And Daedalus, although a clever and cunning inventor laughed at the King's words, and vowed to have her for his own. And so he met with her in the gardens where she gathered produce for the evening table. She smiled at him and then spoke.

You are an extraordinary man. Like me you make a home here amongst these strangers. You believe you walk freely and that I am a slave, but I believe you are as trapped as I. We both find ourselves here against our will and we both use our skills to gain the King's favour.

Reaching into her basket she held out a tiny fruit, as yellow as the sun. She pulled the flesh apart and flung three tiny stones into the soil at her feet, offering him the flesh, which he found to be as sweet as the honey from the king's hives.

These stones will grow into a strong tree and bear fruit in this foreign soil, just as we will become a family, you my husband, I your wife. I will bear you a son and he will grow strong as the fruit tree flourishes. Together we will make this place our own. Together we will turn the tides against this island.

She took his hand and lifted it to her mouth for the fruit was succulent and had coated his fingers with its juice.

And so it was that Icarus was born. A perfect child, in the image of his father. And Naucrate was happy for she believed that through her son she could gain true liberty once more. Daedalus believed that he would never lose the favour of the King, but his wife warned him that a woman would be his downfall, for she could see that just as she had bewitched him so any woman who set her mind to it could persuade the foolish man to do her bidding.

Now Queen Pasiphae, wife to Minos, became enamoured of a Great White Bull. She begged Daedalus to build her a disguise that she might meet with it.

I have seen your work Daedalus, the skill with which you craft your pieces. I have seen the great bird which watches over your lovely wife and keeps guard over your son. I know that you can build me a spectacular beast of my own, as elegant as the bull is strong.

And Daedalus, afraid that she would give up his secrets to the King, for the bird was his most treasured piece, and flattered that she believed in him, agreed to make her beast for her. It would be his masterpiece. And Naucrate cried out.

You will rue the day, my husband, you agreed to work for the Queen, for am I not your mistress and no other? Is Minos not your lord? And now you fool, you conspire against us both and I tell you it will be our downfall.

And so it was. Pasiphae had her way, met with the Bull and bore a gruesome child, the Minotaur, a creature half man, half beast. The King cast out his queen and charged Daedalus to build the labyrinth to enslave the beast. The King's heart was darkened against the man he believed had lived to serve him and he vowed there would be no second chance. Should Daedalus cross him one more time he would pay dearly.

Now at this time Minos demanded tithes of Athens, to safeguard the people from his armies. This beast, the Minotaur, craved the flesh of men, and so Minos called on Athens to send young men and virgins to appease it. Young Theseus offered himself as sacrifice, intent to kill the beast and put an end to the dreadful suffering of his people. When she set her eyes upon him, the lovely Ariadne, daughter to the King, fell instantly in love.

Oh Daedalus, I know you are wise and good, I know you hold great secrets in your mind. I beg you, for the sake of love, show me the secret of your labyrinth. Let me lead my love to safety, that we may be together.

And Daedalus hearing her words agreed to impart the secret. This he kept from Naucrate, fearing what she would say. But Naucrate sent his seeing bird to watch her husband. Too late, the damage done, the beast slain, Theseus escaped. Minos flew into a rage and knowing Daedalus to be at fault had him thrown into his own labyrinth and sealed it up, and with him his young son. When Naucrate heard what had passed, she fell on her knees before the king.

My lord I beg you, not my son. Take that fool Daedalus and let him rot for he has cheated us both, you his lord and I his mistress. Let my son free.

Minos looked down upon the woman, still as graceful and more beautiful than any he had ever known and he felt great pleasure at her plight, for she had always been so much aloof. She alone had been beyond the taking and yet here she lay, her head on his feet. What better revenge could there be on that crude craftsman than to take his own wife?

I will consider your plight Naucrate, for I have known you since a girl and you still please me greatly. You have such beauty and such wisdom for one who comes from other shores, in fact no woman from our shores has graced this island quite as you have. Give yourself to me freely and I will grant your son his freedom.

And so Naucrate went with Minos although her heart was breaking, for to lie with this king was to lie with her captor, who she had vowed to overthrow. And while they lay together Daedalus and his son plotted their escape. They fashioned wings of wax and feathers, and leapt from the highest tower. Young Icarus, against his father's cries, soared high in the sky to feel the freedom his mother had told him of, to taste the air she had promised he would breathe. And as he flew he called out to her that he was free now and would return to claim her and take her with him, and as he soared his father's cries were lost and then as he grew closer to the sun, his wings caught fire and down he fell.

Naucrate's cries could be heard across the island, a wailing so great that the waves stopped on the shore. The tides ceased from that day on, the sea bound to the island just as she was. And Minos, knowing that her heart was broken, took her in his arms. And when he looked into her eyes he saw her look of loss and knew she never could be his.

I thought I would be content to have you as my own, but now I see that I have broken you. I cannot keep you here against your will. Your beauty pains me, for what is your beauty to me without your love? And just as I am at fault for the loss of your son, so is your husband and I vow now to find him and bring him back, for if I must witness your pain so must he. You have truly been an honest wife, without guile and malice, unlike my own adulterous queen. I will avenge the death of your son and win forgiveness, I will bring back Daedalus and make him suffer for what he has done.

Had he turned to look again he would have seen her smiling. Because inside, she felt a life, a new beginning. These men were fools, Daedalus and the King. They had caused her to lose her only love, her first-born son. Yet with this new life growing inside her, she could begin again and bring about the downfall of them both. She raised her eyes towards the sky and cried out to the ancients who ruled her homeland.

Oh Father and Mother, hear me, Naucrate your daughter. Right the wrongs which have befallen me here on this dreadful island. I offer you my unborn son, that he may avenge the death of his brother and bring about the downfall of the fathers. Let his brother's father and his own father die. Let him watch over these people and learn their secrets, just as the great bird, built by my husband, watched over me. Let his father's people be his slaves just I was once his father's slave. Let him find a queen to match my strength and honour and may they rule together in love to carry on my name.

And the Ancients heard her plea. The ancient mothers granted the unborn child power and vision, to rule the people as he wished and agreed that he would find the perfect mate. But the ancient fathers, angered by their brazen daughter Naucrate, who had plotted against men for her own end, devised their own agreement. Wings they gave the child, unlike his brother's pale and waxen efforts, but strong and black, to take him swiftly from sea to mountain, half man half bird they made him. And although the island people would be his slaves, he in turn would be enslaved, to the island itself, doomed to walk its shores for all eternity, unable to cross the sea to other lands. And this island would suffer at the hands of invaders and these people would be tried at every generation. So Naucrate had begged, so would it be. Let her son live out his life on foreign soil. No island girl would be his mate and none would match his mother, for Naucrate was of noble blood and only her bloodline would set him free."

The girl set the book down and smiled at me, "a good story, yes?" My mind raced over the stories my mother had told me.

"And these island people have suffered at the hands of invaders it is true. There has been much suffering here, many deaths, many atrocities."

"And do you know anything else about Naucrate? About

her second son?"

"No, my area of research is the Jewish community which once flourished here."

"But what about the son," I asked, " half bird half man?"

"I am employed here as a historian, of more recent times," the girl's demeanour changed slightly. "Did you know that during the occupation the Jews of Crete were herded into boats, which never reached the mainland? I study the real tragedies of this place. These things you speak of are mythologies from the ancient times, particular to this island. There is a man, an American who lives here, he knows much about the superstitions and mythology which surrounds the island. I am not from here, much of it is localised mythology, spread by word of mouth, an oral history, you understand?"

"Of course," I said, blushing as I noticed the girl check her watch, "I've kept you long enough."

"The man, he visits most days.."

"Oh yes, I think I may have met him, he has an English wife?"

"Perhaps. His name is Douglas, Douglas Winter, like the season!" She laughed at her own observation.

"Thank you," I offered my hand, the girl smiled and took it, shaking it heartily.

"No problem."

I walked outside and stood contemplating my next move, then made my way towards a bench, to sit for while.

"Well you've flushed me out!" I drew myself back from my thoughts. My mother's face, Naucrate, the bird-son, the suffering the island had endured. "Well girl, you've flushed me out! My secret hideaway." I focussed to see Doug, beaming in front of me. I looked blankly at him. "The library? Don't tell Al, she thinks I'm with my drinking buddies!"

"I found a picture, in a book. In the library," I turned to point back at the building.

"Ah, the slave Naucrate, none more beautiful than she."

"You know about her?"

"My subject area hon."

"Why didn't you tell me?"

"Tell you what? That a picture in a book looks a bit like your mum?"

"That she, that my father." I stopped. "You're right, it's just a picture isn't it? And the story, did you read that?"

"Well it took me longer than an afternoon. Check you out, here a few days and already the expert. I spent weeks boning up on my language skills to translate that, once I'd found it. It's written in a very old style. How did you manage it?"

"The librarian read it to me."

"Lucky you."

"Is that who you think my dad is, Doug? Half man half bird, second son of the slave Naucrate?"

"It's a story, like all stories. They get passed on, changed. Maybe your dad knew the story, maybe he'd seen the picture, maybe he thought it was funny to use it to chat up girls?"

"And that's what you think?"

"I'm looking at all the myths and legends from this place, how they get passed from family to family. I'm checking solid facts, dates and events with stories told by local people."

"Do you think my mother believed it?" I pressed him, "Doug?"

"I think she believed a lot of stuff about your dad," he hung his head and shifted his weight from one leg to the other.

"And what about you?"

"Al says that he used your mum's vulnerability, he told her stories to freak her out. To keep her where he wanted her."

"And what do you think?" I repeated, "What do you think Doug?"

"Shit Ally, I don't know," Doug looked straight at me again, "the longer you stay here the more you start to believe anything. Let's get a coffee and talk."

The windows are wide open. From where I lie on the couch, I can hear the sounds that comfort me. Cicadas singing, the gentle chatter of the chickens scratching away outside, an insect buzzing at the window. If I turn my head I can see the branches of the lemon trees brushing against the shutters. I swing my legs off the edge of the bed. It is a high iron bedstead, painted white. The bed cover is woven from delicate lace and a rug is thrown across the foot of the bed, made from that fibre which smells so strongly of him, dark green and soft. When I hold it to my face, or wrap it around me I feel as if he is wrapping his arms around me and keeping me safe. The place has an air of antiquity about it, strange for a man's house. I love it. So far removed from the furniture on display in the windows of the stores in town. Brazen pieces. High sheen veneer, marble and onyx, gold trim, leather couches, ornate mirrors and elaborate light fittings. It is simplicity here. Wooden staircase with well-worn tread and handrail, cold stone floors, shutters thick with the paint of years. The kitchen has an old fridge and a simple stove which runs off a massive gas bottle which stands behind it. The wood burner has an oven in it and we have a brick built oven outside in the courtyard. This is my home. I feel the chill of the floor spreading through my feet, pleasing to feel the cool stone. As I walk downstairs I hear the familiar sound of his bike as it coasts into the courtyard. I hear the chickens scatter, and as I look out of the window at the turn of the stairs, I see one of those birds in the trees lift itself into the air on massive polished wings. I run to meet him and throw my arms around him as he walks through the door.

"Rai Anna." He lifts me and holds me tight and I breathe in as deeply as I can to hold the scent of him inside me.

"You're early. I was bored," I mumble into his chest. He strokes my hair and lifts my face to look at me.

"How, bored? Your are free to do what you please here."

The word jars.

It taunts me.

I am not free.

I wait for him to come back. That sense of being watched never leaves me. If I walk beyond the courtyard, towards the neighbouring farm I stop and turn to look back, expecting to find somebody following me. When I wander from room to room in the house I am afraid I will find a secret and he will know and be angry. Suddenly I do not feel at home, the feeling is gone, just as soon as I heard that simple word, 'free'.

"I have no purpose."

"Purpose?" He is laughing at me. "My beautiful Anna needs purpose. Am I not your purpose?"

"Don't tease me."

"No you are right. I hoped that my child would give you purpose, but.." His face hardens. His lids fall heavily across his eyes.

I'm losing him again. I wait, expecting him to be angry. Each month I hope I can give him the news he wants to hear. And each time we make love that voice inside my head says CAREFUL WHAT YOU WISH FOR. Perhaps it is my fault. Perhaps my reservation is what holds my body back. Perhaps I am willing my body to reject him. And if he knew this what would he do to me?

"You do want my child, Anna?" He's inside my head again.

"Of course. More than anything." And that is true. I do want his child more than anything. If I gave him a child he would know that I loved him and he would trust me and allow me to breathe and we would be so happy. SHUT UP. To the voice inside. YOU DON'T KNOW WHAT I WANT. SHUT UP. "More than anything." And I nestle into him like his daughter will when she is born.

"What if you took a job?"

"You wouldn't mind? It's just that Al.." He holds his hand up to silence me.

"Why bother with her?" He takes my hands in his and turns them palm up. "I cannot have these doing scrubbing and peeling for that woman. I know a job for you." Before I can say any more

163

he continues, "so you have a car, so you can do this job. My friend Vassilis has a travel company. You will work for him. It is easy. Just to drive to the villas and deliver the laundry for the maids, or provisions for the tourists. It will be fun for you, no hard work, no late nights. No trouble for you. And I can find you and we can take lunch together. I know all of Vassilis' houses, I can show you."

Doug pulled me towards a table set underneath the trees in the square. The cloth was dusty from the sandy flooring and from the cars driving past. He waved to a waiter to come and serve them.

"Not very peaceful, sorry, but we won't get bothered here, it's mainly cab drivers and old men drink here." He waited quietly until the waiter had returned with their order.

"Here, tuck in, you look a bit pale," he pushed a meze across the table to me and helped himself to a prawn. "Ouzo. Yia mas!" He raised a glass to me and waited for me to drink mine. I held it up to my nose and inhaled.

"Liquorice."

"Do you the world of good, stick some water in if you like, take the edge off it." I tipped in some water and sipped. The liquid slid softly down to my belly where it rested in a glow.

"Mm. Not bad."

"So. Do I think your dad is the son of Naucrate, imprisoned on this island? Do I think he is half-man half-bird? Do I think he is the vrykolakas? Or maybe the vrykolakas stories came about because of Naucrate's unfortunate second son? Heck of a lot to take in."

I picked through the food on the plate in front of me, trying to find something to tempt my appetite. Doug waited, then tried again.

"I think your mom believed a lot of the stories."

"And how about you?"

"Well you tell me Ally, what do you think about your mom?"

"I told you, she always told stories. Some of them fit in with this stuff today, although I can't remember it all, the business with the sea, not being able to cross it. But to be honest I think maybe she just got depressed, you know, post natal, it happens all the time doesn't it? A woman on her own out here, cut off from her friends, like you said, she could start believing anything. Sometimes I worry she is really mad and that means I might be too."

"Al is right about one thing, Anna had no problems when we first met her, your mom's not mad honey. Depression? Maybe you're right," Doug hesitated and I touched his hand, sensing he had more to say. I prompted, "but?"

"But nothing! Just that your dad was, is, a strong character and I believe he would never give up on you. Be careful where you go and who you see, things aren't always what they seem here."

"And what now? Where do I go from here?"

"Meet us at Costas' this afternoon, we'll see what Al's unearthed. I got a proper translation of that Naucrate myth, maybe not the same as the version you've just heard, but it'll give you the gist of it, to read over. I'll drop a copy off at your room, don't tell Alison, she freaks about all that stuff when I talk about it. Maybe there's clues in that. If your mom did come to believe it all, then maybe it'll tell you where to look next."

Somewhere between my old life and the new one, these mornings belong to me. The car piled high with laundry and boxes of provisions for new clients, I turn off the coastal road and head up the hill. There are a few tavernas here and bars which service the villas and apartments built for the tourists. Vassilis, my new boss, favours old properties, off the beaten track. Today I am looking for a farm building which he's converted into two, one part to house a family, the other just right for a couple. I drive with one hand on the wheel, the other clutching the directions and a hand drawn map to explain the exact position. At the brow of the hill, just before the road sweeps round to the left I spot the entrance, overhung by bright pink bougainvillea. Those paper-thin blossoms, each one weightless, but the bough seems laden. I pull the car up under a lemon tree. Breathe in. The brochure boasts this. An old stone built farm house in a secluded spot, three kilometres from the village, a well-stocked garden with lemon trees, pomegranates, bougainvillea, even an old well and a view across the valley, leading down to the coast.

I select a key from the bundle, slipping each around the ring, reading the labels until I find the right one. I carry the box of groceries into the house and busy myself emptying the contents into the fridge and onto the counter in the kitchen. I look for a good place to lean the customary welcome letter for the new guests. I notice a cafetiere, such a foreign object in this traditional kitchen, then I see the electric kettle, another interloper. In the kitchen drawer will be a potato peeler, a garlic press, a potato masher, small concessions to the English clientele who frequent these houses. I fill a vase with water and go outside again to cut some of the blossoms to add a dash of pink to the white interior, then carry them through to the bedroom, check the beds are made properly, turn down the sheets, *close the shutters, but leave the windows open to air the place. Slip a mosquito tablet into the machine plugged into the socket. Perfect. I sit for a moment outside and imagine that it is I who have arrived for a holiday. I am unloading my bags, discovering the food parcels left for my first night, fat tomatoes cut from the vine, a juicy cucumber, Lipton tea bags, long life milk, matches, a loaf of bread. I am turning to my husband to say, 'oh look, lemon trees'. But I have lemon trees of my own, I have a garden like this and breathe this air every day and wake up to these sounds and this heat. I am the lucky one because I live this life. Then above the sound of the cicadas I hear a harsh caw, from the trees beyond the garden. A crow sits watching me. It shakes its head at me, before lifting off over the trees towards the mountains. Another calls back from a distance.*

I look around at the scene again. The life I lead bears no resemblance to this at all. I do not take delight in the lemons in the trees at the house in the mountains. I have no husband to please, but a dark man, a creature who changes as soon as I think I know what he is. I will never sit and read the latest novel, browse through the harbour's tourist shops. I will never choose to go to the beach for the day, or drink cocktails in the new cafés in the town. I do as he tells me and go where he takes me. Even this job is one he has found me, with his people. The crow calls again, far off.

"Yar- soo". A woman is walking towards me, down the pathway. English I am sure. Her shoulders are pink, burned from the sun. She is holding a booklet in her hand, a guide book, no a brochure. She wears a pair of sandals with Velcro fastenings, three quarter length trousers in a khaki colour with a pretty sleeveless blouse in a similar shade. Beyond her is a rental car, a man at the wheel. He wears a straw hat, a panama. I smile, thinking that they'll appreciate the cafetiere and the garlic press. She is waving at me as she walks.

"Para-cal-owe" she pronounces the words awkwardly. "I say, excuse me," she waves again. I open my mouth to speak, but I have forgotten the words. I watch as she fumbles through her book, searching for the right page. She holds it up to me and points at a picture of the house.

"Eth-owe?" She points repeatedly at the picture. "Eth-owe? Here? This house? Vassilis' House?"

"She might not be from here darling." The man calls from the car, "Try French."

I open my mouth again, but something has caught in my throat, an insect or a leaf, a feather. My hand goes up to feel my neck, but it is not my hand, sharp fingers close tight. Slim and black, sharp nails clutch at me. I cannot breathe. HELP ME. She doesn't notice and pushes her face closer to mine.

"Can I be of some assistance?" I know the voice and look up to see Korakas walking down the path, calling, but he doesn't look at me. He doesn't see this thing that is choking me in front of them all. He stops at the car and calls to the woman, "Can I be of some assistance?" The woman rushes to show him the brochure.

"Thank you so much. My husband has got us quite lost!" The man in the car rolls his eyes. "I'm sure we're quite lost. We're looking for this," she thrusts the brochure at Korakas and he takes her hand in his.

"Madam. You are quite safe and your husband has brought you to the right place. This is my friend Vassillis' House." He turns, still holding her hand in his and gestures towards the house where I am standing.

"Madam your new home, for as long as you desire," and he drops his head in a bow. The husband stares straight ahead, unimpressed. The woman flushes and fans herself with the brochure. The claws have gone and I drop my hand to my side, but still I can't speak or move. Korakas turns to me and says something I don't understand. He leads the woman past me into the house. The man rolls the car slowly down the slope and parks outside the house and I watch as he carries their luggage inside. Korakas appears again, shaking the man's hand and bowing his head slightly.

"Enjoy my friend. Enjoy your stay."

"Oh!" The man calls after Korakas, "should we tip the maid?"

"The maid?" Korakas looks to me and laughs, "Oh no my friend. I will take care of the maid!" As he reaches me he takes me by the elbow and steers me up the path to where he has parked his motorbike.

"How could you?" Now the words come gushing out. " How could you make me look like such a fool?" I have tears in my eyes and he is laughing.

" Rai Anna, I did no such thing."

"Calling me the maid!" I shake his hand off me.

"It was for fun. Let them think what they like."

"I'm English! Just like them!"

"Not so like them, eh Anna? You are becoming less like them every day you spend here with me." He swings his leg over the bike and kicks it into life. "Will you ride with me?"

"No, my car's still down there." I jerk my head towards it but my body feels heavy and my feet set in the ground again.

"Come drive with me, one of Vassillis' boys will bring your car later. Sit on the back here with me and hold me. I will show you a beach where these tourists never go."

Walking down the back streets, I tried to imagine what it must have been like when the town was first built, and before that. What lay here in the days when Naucrate walked the island, if she ever did? And if the wings of Icarus were in fact sails of a ship, perhaps the labyrinth was nothing more than the twisting turning streets of the town, and if that were true, perhaps Naucrate's second son was just a boy after all, with no more power or magic than any other. I stopped walking and turned, certain that somebody was behind me. Nothing. A mangy cat on a step hissed, then stretched and moved on. I felt uneasy. Back in England I had always been certain that my mother's stories were just that. But here, the people, even the places, harboured secrets. Every street, every square could have been the site of some ancient tragedy. And what about Xenon? Appearing from nowhere, knowing my whereabouts at all times, knowing my thoughts it seemed. My head ached, whether with the ouzo or with the thoughts banging away inside I wasn't sure. Hurrying now, I worked my way through the streets back to the peace of my room.

The beach stretches out below us, shallow pools of water pale blue and green against the sand.

'It's beautiful.' I lean against him and close my eyes, enjoying the scent of him and holding the image of the place in my head.

"It was more beautiful, but now we have to share it, they come and destroy it little by little."

"Who?"

"The tourists of course, look at them." His face has hardened again, those furrows across his brow, his eyes small and black. The dirt track widens into a natural car park. Cars and motorbikes parked haphazardly. In the dunes couples lie sunbathing, a carrier bag skuttles past like tumble weed, carried by the breeze. "In my mother's time this sand was coral pink, bright against the turquoise of the sea which lapped at the shore. And now. Like the people, it has faded, sacrificed its splendour to appease the appetites of the incomers."

I know better than to interrupt him. When he talks about his mother he is morose. The disappointment of his childhood weighs heavy on him and although I have tried to break through I always fail. I walk a little way off and watch the people who arrive, stand and take photographs. I feel isolated from them. I am not one of them and yet I am not an islander.

A man is poking at a fire and lays some small fish across a grill. I feel bile rise to my throat and swallow it down. He is beside me, concerned. "You are unwell?" His face is soft again. "Anna?"

"I just felt a bit sick, that's all. I'm fine."

"You should drink, it is hot today. But not here, I will take you to a quiet place, without all these people." He passes me a bottle of water from the back of the bike and waits for me to drink before we drive off again.

I wanted to dip my feet in the water, to feel the cool sea against my skin. I wanted to run the pink sand through my fingers, but what he wants is to show me his island and then move on. He never rests, never waits, and so I must move on with him.

The telephone on the bedside table rang and I leant across to answer it. A package had arrived for me, the receptionist said. The translation from Doug, I thought. Although parts of the story were clear in my mind, there were things which I had missed, how could the son break the curse? Would he grow old? Would his mother walk the island with him? I grabbed the key from the table and locked the door behind me. Having the story to think about distracted me from the disappearance of my mother, as if unravelling this story was the key to finding out exactly where she had gone. The receptionist, a girl with flawless skin and immaculate clothes, nails polished with the palest of pink varnish, handed me a small parcel. Not the translation I had expected at all. I opened it to discover a small punnet of fruit, tiny yellow plums.

The receptionist laughed, "despila!" I sniffed one and bit into it, the woman shrieked, "no, no, you must wash! These fruits are dirty, they grow only in the village here. A love token," she laughed again, but I dropped the plum back into the box, the sweetness of its flesh still coating my lips.

"A love token?"

"It's what the village girls believe, if a boy offers you this and you eat it from his hand, you are his forever. It's very village," she shook her head in obvious disapproval of anything 'village'. "I don't believe such a thing."

"Who left this here?" I asked the girl, who flicked her head upwards and puckered her lips in a nonchalant dismissal,

"I don't know."

"And has anything else been left for me?" The girl tutted, the familiar signal for 'no'. I licked my lips as I walked back round to my room behind the hotel, clutching the box of fruit to me, tempted to take out another and try the flesh again.

"The sweetest fruit," Xenon waiting at the door, astride his motorbike, "from my village." I flushed, angry at my excitement in seeing him.

"You sent me this?" I thrust the box at him and he grabbed my arm.

"I needed to see you. Why have you kept away?

"That doesn't usually stop you from popping up! Anyway, I've been busy."

"With your English friends? I pulled my arm away from his grasp, "What I do and who I see is my own business."

"Alithea, you should know by now, this is a small town and the people talk, talk. It's the only sport they have. Nothing here is your own business. Come, ride with me and I'll take you away from them all."

I relaxed my grip on the box. His shirt was open at the neck and I caught a glimpse of the cord which held that ring, so like my own and my mother's. I hesitated, then spoke, being careful to soften my voice.

"Well I could do with a change of scenery." I flicked my eyes up to watch his reactions, when I had flirted before he had withdrawn from me. I calculated just how willing I should appear. He looked at me and studied my face, then traced the line of my arm from shoulder to wrist and wrapped his fingers around it.

"Come then." He started the motorbike with a kick and nodded at me to jump on. I hesitated for just a second.

"You will be safe," he teased.

"Oh yes, I know," I laughed, but inside I didn't know at all.

The harbour stinks, it makes me gag. He laughs when I tell him.

"Good, perhaps you will be happy to stay home with me."
He is thrilled and I am afraid. We tried for this so hard and now it's a reality I worry that I've made a terrible mistake. What kind of a child will we make?

Last night I dreamed it had wings and when it cried it cawed like a bird, harsh and loud. When I tried to hold it, it scratched me. I don't tell him this, just that I feel tired and sick. In the mornings he will hold my head while I hang over the sink retching. He strokes my hair and wets a cloth for my face. He kisses me and whispers words I don't understand. He laughs and smiles. I have made him happy and his mood has lightened, but I feel trapped.

WHAT HAVE I DONE?

He has me now.

Vassilis tells me he doesn't need me to work, the season is all but done. I know this is for Korakas, not me. The woman who bears his child must not work, she must eat well and rest.

I sit in the courtyard and watch the chickens as they scratch in the dirt. This will be my life too, scratching out my existence, raising a child. The chickens scatter as one of the black birds swoops down to pick up a scrap from the ground. It cocks its head at me and I kick my foot at it to shoo it away.

"Leave me alone!" I shout at it. I'm tired of his shabby birds watching me all the time. It hops sideways but continues to strut around the yard, then slowly lifts itself up into the air back to its vantage point in the tree beyond the gates.

Inside the house is cool. I wander from room to room, looking out of each window in turn. There are no curtains, shutters keep out the darkness of the night or the sun during the day. The paint is peeling, revealing soft wood beneath. As I pass each window

I look for the birds. They do not favour the lemon trees with their low hanging branches, they prefer to sit high up and watch me.

"Watching the birds watching you again?" He teases me.

"You made me jump."

"They called me back, told me my woman was lonely, walking room to room."

"Don't make fun of me, I'm just keeping cool inside the house."

He pulls me close and strokes my hair. I feel the warmth of him and close my eyes. When the baby comes he will love us both, keep us close.

WHAT HAVE I DONE?

I sat upright as we drove through the town, I caught an old woman looking at me and my face flushed with shame. It had taken me very little time here to realise that things had not changed so much from my mother's days, a young girl on the back of a man's motorbike was still cause for disapproval amongst the older generation. I sat with my hands on my thighs, feigning ease at being so close to him.

As the bike climbed out of the town towards the main highway, I wrapped my arms around Xenon's chest and leant into his back. The smell of him made me anxious, that cold fresh smell. Christmas, my mother said. Surrounded by my friends, opening my presents on my birthday, that scarf, the one I took everywhere, the colour, the odour. I breathed in the familiar scent of Xenon. The same.

"Shall we go to your house?" As nonchalant as I could, my thoughts catching at my tongue like brambles pulling at my clothes, my fears lying hidden, for me to trip and stumble over. He did not reply, but clicked the bike through the gears as we sped up the road towards the highway, then across it to join the mountain road. Once the bike was climbing, he relaxed and held one of his arms across mine for a moment.

There is something about the place when the tourists have gone. The pace of life has slowed right down. The sun sets a little faster each day. We used to time it some days, sitting in the harbour sharing a beer. That was before, when I was part of the ex-pat crew. Now I am part of, well I am part of him, our new family. My waist is thickening and my clothes are tight. He doesn't seem to notice. He seems content, but I am lonely. Some days he is away from first light, he says he has to review his land.

"Can't we stay in the house in the harbour, so that I can be nearer my friends?" I ask him, "and closer to the clinic for my check ups?" He laughs at me.

" The air is clean in the village. But if you are bored I will take you on a trip."

He throws our bags into the back of the truck and helps me into the cab. I pull my scarf around me, the sun is bright but sometimes the wind catches me and I feel the cold. We join the Ethniki and head west. Before long he turns off the main road and we begin to climb the mountain route. He talks very little, but pats my knee from time to time, smiles. Asks me if I am okay, or hungry.

"Where are we going?"

"To the far side of the island, it is quiet. A good place to be." I sleep a little I think, because now we are driving down, winding down the mountainside, this way and that. Below us is a bleak landscape, rocky and uncultivated. The sea is grey and blue in swirling patches.

"Africa!" He laughs as he points. "North Africa, across the sea, not so very far from us after all."

He continues to drive carefully, as he drops towards sea level. There are only a few houses here, small dwellings. In the distance I see a ruined building, a fortress, with a round turret. The road towards the coast stretches across the plain. Three figures bent double are at the roadside a little farther on, village women. They straighten up as we pass and I see that they've been collecting horta, wild greens. The stuff is supposed to be a delicacy, but I find it bitter, like dandelions, picked for my dad, fleshy stems running with white juice, 'you'll wet the bed!' I hear him say.

The truck pulls into a car park next to a taverna. It doesn't look as if it's open. The box sign swings from its chain, unlit. The door is closed. We walk around the side and sit down at one of the tables closest to the beach. I love to hear the sea again. The tables are under a thatched canopy, brown from the season's sun. The plastic table coverings are dusty. There is a sense of abandonment about the place. I don't like it.

"What's wrong?" In my thoughts again.

"It's a bit creepy, that's all."

"Creepy?"

"You know, scary, dark."

"Dark yes. This place has a dark history." He stands up and calls out for someone to come. A man slides open a door and comes out to serve us. He shuffles slowly towards the table and flicks a cloth across it, unsettling the dust. Korakas snaps at him and the man calls over his shoulder. A woman appears at the door, she too snaps at the man and proceeds to wipe the table with a damp cloth. She clucks and smiles at me, patting her stomach as she does, then, glancing at Korakas, she crosses herself and shuffles back inside again.

I sip my drink through a straw, sharp, cloudy lemonade from a glass bottle, sugary sweet. The woman returns with a tray of food. Dark greens floating in a slick of olive oil with boiled potatoes sitting on the top. She gestures, lifting her fingers to her mouth and smiling, "fye, fye," encouraging me to eat the stuff. Patting her belly and pointing at mine. I smile and nod at her, but I have no intention of eating the stuff, the look of it makes my stomach turn over. I pick at some bread and eat most of the salad, with big red chunks of tomatoes and lumps of feta cheese, and manage some grilled pork.

"I will save you from yiayia, pass me the horta."

He sprinkles the plate of greens and potatoes with salt and when he has finished it he pushes the plate back over to my side of the table so that the old woman will think I have eaten it. We grin like conspiring teenagers.

"It's beautiful here."

"Now it is beautiful? First it was," he hesitates, "creepy?" He tries out the word and smiles in satisfaction at himself.

"It's beautiful because I am here with you." I wonder at myself sometimes. I say things, words just come out. But he's smiling, I have made him happy, he believes me.

He throws some money on the table and pulls me to my feet. He calls out for the old woman again and she appears wiping her hands on a towel. She leads us to a stairway and produces a key from her pocket. As she opens the door at the top of the stairs, she pats my cheek and smiles.

The room inside is large and airy, with a bed against the back wall. Framed by the window is a view across the scrub land to the beach and then ocean. The sea stretches for miles, into a light mist at the horizon. If I look to the left I can see the fortress below us. This place is desolate, there seems to be only one other taverna, a few houses, a few goats. Nothing else.

"Come," he pulls me away from the window and on to the bed and strokes my hair. "My Anna, here we can have rest and peace together, without distraction."

When I wake, he is not at my side. The window is open. A heavy mist has come in off the sea and swirls around the fortress, floating above the ground.

"Spirits are abroad." He appears from the balcony, already dressed with his coat thrown around his shoulders. He speaks again. "Spirits of the warriors." I shiver. He frightens me with his stories. "They serve that other king. But as my blood line continues they will become weak and have no place here." He turns to me and opens his coat inviting me to him. "Come and see." I hesitate. "Do not be afraid. It is only mist that comes in from the sea." Then he throws his coat around me, pulls me close to his chest, wraps me in his huge black wings.

We coasted down the track, the chain on the bike clicking as we bumped across dry earth. I held tight, involuntarily, until we came to a stop.

"It's a lovely house," I said. "You're very lucky."

"Lucky?" He pulled his brows together.

"To have such a restful place to come," I looked around at the old walls, the lemon trees, the crumbling storehouse, and the chickens.

Chickens, flapping and clucking, a woman jumping over them in her haste, running, calling out.

Xenon sighed, interrupting my thoughts, and rolled his motorbike to the side of the courtyard and leant it on its stand.

"Sometimes it is very lonely out here." He turned his back to me and looked up to the mountains. A bird squawked in the trees beyond the wall and I looked across to see one of those big black ravens settling in the branches. Xenon picked a fallen lemon from the ground and hurled it at the bird, missing by a mile.

"Fige!" He yelled at it.

"Bloody birds," I said, almost to myself, a pang of realisation as I spoke the words my mother had used so many times.

"Yes, bloody birds," he was laughing now, "bloody, bloody birds, always spying!" I shivered, and he walked towards me with his arms out stretched.

"Alithea. Come." He put his arm around my shoulder and walked me towards the door of the house. "Let's eat."

"Eat, eat, that's all you ever do," I tried to be light, but I felt anxious. When he touched me I felt a combination of fear and excitement, not fear of him, I was sure he meant me no harm, but fear of what might happen.

> *In the dentist's chair, the smell of clean things, the sound of water in the little fountain at my side, pink and inviting, a calming voice, wanting my mum.*

He smiled at me and we went inside. I watched him as he opened the fridge to investigate what was inside. Some cheese, olives, bread wrapped in a cloth on the side, some fat, misshapen tomatoes, dark cured meat which he cut into chunks and an old lemonade bottle filled with wine. He fed me mouthful, by mouthful, and we drank the wine greedily.

"This olive comes from my trees on the other side of the mountains, this olive has seen across the ocean to Africa." I bit into it, from his fingers. He selected a piece of cheese. "And this cheese," he popped it into my mouth,

"What has the cheese seen?" I teased.

"The inside of my goat's belly!"

"You have a goat?"

"I have many goats, they graze on the shore of the lake not far from where your mother first lived." He dropped the piece of meat he had been poised to feed to me and his face hardened, his eyes blackened as he looked towards the door.

I took a breath, my stomach feeling light, my head buzzing from the wine.

"How do you know where my mother lived?"

"I told you," he snapped, "talk, talk, it is all these people do. I told you also that I would make enquiries about your mother, to help you, to help you find your mother, if indeed she had returned." I stretched my hand across the table to touch his,

"Yes you did, of course. Thank you." He pushed his chair back and stood up. "Please! Don't go!" I held my hand out to him and he dropped to his knees by my side.

"Alithea," he rested his head in my lap, "this place makes me crazy." I stroked his hair, silky and thick on top and soft like down around his neck, the light fell across it and it glistened dark black. He groaned with pleasure and looked up at me. "Alithea, you are so beautiful." I laughed, embarrassed. He stood up and lifted me towards him, holding my chin with one hand. "My beautiful Alithea," he leaned towards me and touched my lips lightly with his, holding me there for a moment.

DEAR GOD! I felt myself falling, my head ached, I could hear the sounds of the day around me, cicadas, chickens, could smell him, fresh and cold, could feel the heat of him against me, taste the wine on his lips. I let him lead me to the stairs and let my hand trail on the wooden banister, worn smooth with years of use, each step as worn as the handrail. I wondered how many feet had trodden them and who they had belonged to. He pulled me, insistent now, into a light room. The smell of him gave way to a floral scent and I noticed that the jasmine which grew up the side of the house was tumbling in through the open window. The room was bare, but for a tall cupboard, a table in front of the window with a chair at its side and a large bed. Xenon pushed me onto the bed and turned to take something from a bowl on the table. He lay next to me and held his hand up to my mouth.

"Eat it," he said, as he tore the tiny fruit apart, then offered me the flesh.

"Despila," I whispered, closing my eyes.

"From a tree on my land higher in the mountains."
He threw the tiny flat sided stones onto the floor and licked the juice which had trickled down my chin. The fruit was sweet, slippery, like mango or passion fruit. I arched my back and opened my mouth slightly to accept more, but Xenon leapt from the bed.

"What? What is it?" Xenon strode across the room to the window. I heard cawing from the trees outside, then a man's voice calling, from below.

"I must go, wait for me. Please wait. You will be safe here."

"But where are you going?"

I ached, my head ached, my body ached.

"Don't leave me, not now." I pulled at him to stay, but he took my hands and held them at my sides and whispered to me.

"I will be back. I need you, I need you to stay here."
He touched my face again as the man outside called again.
"Nai, endaxi!" Xenon shouted back, then turned and left.

Now my dreams are more real than my daily life. I am in a garden. I watch from the trees. I am a bird. I see everything. I hear a woman calling, shouting for her husband, calling him 'fool'. Some nights I hear her crying, begging

–not my son, let my son free!

I wake crying too, wishing she could have my child in place of her own. One night I watch her wade into the sea and shout against the wind, desperate. I tell him my dreams.

"I am having a boy and I am going to lose him to this island."

"Ssh, koukla," he strokes my face. "Our child will grow strong and happy, she will be like you, brave and good. We shall have a daughter and she will be the strength of us both."

He seems so certain that I try and forget, but again at night I hear the woman crying, I hear how angry she is. Sometimes I hear her calling through the trees, and in the cawing of those birds I can make out her voice, screaming her vengeance on the men who caused the death of her son and offering her next born to make amends.

But today the sun is shining and I sit under the trees, close my eyes. I rest my hand across my belly and feel a kick inside and laugh.

"You are happy." He's beside me again and kneels down to look into my face.

"Yes, I felt the baby kick."

"No!" His face breaks into a smile, light fills his eyes, he reaches his hand out to touch me, then draws it back again. "You are laughing at me. Making fun."

"No!" I take his hand and put it on my side, "here, you feel." We wait, quietly and then the baby kicks again. He pulls his hand away quickly.

"You are doing this!"

"No, it's the baby, try again." He puts his hand on my belly and it kicks again. His smile returns and he lays his head against me and whispers soft words which I can't understand.

"We shall call her Alithea."

"Oh, if it's a girl I wanted to call her.."

"She will be Alithea." He takes his hand away and stands up. I feel cold again. The birds call from the trees and he glances up to look before walking back towards the house.

"Don't walk away!" I shout and run after him. "How dare you tell me what to call my child? What if it's not a girl? Has that bloody doctor told you and not me?"

"Ssh, be calm,"

"I won't be calm!"

"The doctor tells you what he tells me." Those birds are listening, so I pull him inside, I whisper.

"Listen to me, what has he told you?" I know they speak in secret, I know they talk about me and I can't understand the words. He took me to a clinic where nobody I know has been. The best he said, only the best for me. Where I will have a quiet room, the baby taken care of, so I can rest.

"He tells me what he tells you."

"That's not true. He speaks to me like I'm a child, then speaks to you and I can't understand."

"Anna" he strokes my face, "Koukla, he speaks to you as best he can, he speaks to you in your tongue and then addresses me in his, in this way he can be sure that what he said is right, no mistakes have been made."

"So why has he told you it's a girl and not told me?"

"He has not told me. You have seen the pictures every time we go, a face, an arm, fingers, a tiny heart pumping."

Each visit I have a scan, it's what they do because we pay, no waiting, no crowds, each visit we get to look and see how big the baby is, where it lies, its tiny heart beating like a blinking eye. And when the doctor asks if he should tell the sex, Korakas shakes his head and smiles. The clinic is set in a walled garden, a beautiful town house four storeys high. I will have a quiet room, my own bathroom, fresh cooked meals and nurses to take the baby when I'm tired. He strokes my hair again and speaks softly.

"I know that we shall have a daughter and we will call her Alithea which means truth. She will grow strong and beautiful and she will set me free."

And he takes me in his arms and lets me cry. I'm so tired. He lifts me and carries me upstairs to bed and lies with me until I fall asleep.

I'm in the garden, a woman is calling. I'm running through the trees, the ground is soft, I can't find her. If she would just stay still, but she's moving, I think she wants to trick me, she's trying to confuse me.

"Anna!"

I sit up. I'm in bed. The window is open and I hear the voice again,

"Anna? Are you there?" I roll onto my side and drop my feet off the edge of the bed, this damn belly makes me move like an old woman.

"Alison?" She is standing outside looking up, smiling.

"Well? Let me in then!" I manage the stairs as fast as I can and meet her at the door into the courtyard, and fling my arms around her.

"Hey! What a welcome." She pushes me away and takes a look at me. "Where's his Lordship?"

"I don't know, I was sleeping."

"You look like crap, is this what pregnancy really does to you?"

"I don't sleep too well, I dream a lot."

"Yeah, they say that."

"They?"

"Books, you know, pregnancy books. I've been reading up on it."

"Oh, Karen left some books, but I got fed up reading, none of it seems to count here. It all seems to be about somebody else." She pushes me into a chair and opens the fridge door to find *something cold to drink.*

"It's so good to see you."

"Well I'd have come sooner but you know how I get on with your fella!"

"He says I have to call the baby Alithea and now I realise that means she'd be Al, just like you. He chose the name and it's your name! What a laugh. I was so upset but now it seems like the joke's on him."

"What a jerk, he thinks he can tell you what to call your kid? What if it's a boy?"

"He says it won't be. He seems so sure. Maybe we could call it Douglas."

"Bit harsh don't you think? I mean Doug's a sweetie, but I wouldn't inflict the name on a kid."

She makes me laugh with her news while she cooks me some lunch, then we sit under the trees outside, the only sounds, our voices and the cicadas singing. No birds. No eyes watching. She brushes my hair out for me and then plaits it again. She shows me the things she has brought with her, some nappies, a shawl she swears she's knitted, but I know it's the handiwork of some yiayia in town, a tiny fluffy rabbit with a ribbon round its neck. I've had no midwife, no classes, no gifts from friends, but right now I feel like a normal pregnant girl chatting to her friend.

The truck pulls into the yard and Korakas steps out. He doesn't speak until he is standing next to us. I watch him walk, watch his face, the muscles in his neck, the way his hair falls across his face, his head down. He stops and looks straight at Alison. I feel a pain in my side, put my hand against it and press. DON'T BREATHE.

"Ali -son," in that way he has of pronouncing her name. "Kalimera. You keep my Anna amused?" I relax. Alison tosses her hair and lengthens her neck.

"Someone's got to, she'll go potty out here on her own."

"You are right, she should not be alone, but soon she will have our daughter for company."

"I thought we'd go shopping," she turns and looks to me, "you know for baby stuff? I know you've got the basics, but you need some frillies and some stuff for you, it's not all about practicalities you know."

He smiles at me and pulls a roll of notes from his pocket, peels some off, pushing them into my hand.

"Here, takes this, buy what you need and what you don't need. She's right. You should have pretty things, what do I know about this? Go now, it is cooler for you in the evening and we will eat in the harbour when you have finished."

Alison's mouth falls open, "I'm on my bike."

"Well then, take the truck and I will bring your bike down later. I will drive you home Anna, when you are tired." He offers me his hand and leads me to the truck. Alison is silent, for once, but hands him the key to her motorbike.

Once we are in the truck Alison starts, "Oh – my – God!"

"Ssh, wait till we're down the lane." I am laughing, checking in the mirror, he is standing watching as we drive away.

"I cannot believe what just happened! Did the Prince of Darkness actually give you his truck? Did he actually give you money and send you off with me?" We are still laughing when we reach the town. I feel light headed. Ally, my baby, is jumping in my belly, sharing the joke.

I lay on the bed, heard the sound of a truck driving away, down the lane. Outside I could hear the incessant drone of the cicadas and stood up to close the window, but stopped and snapped off a piece of jasmine and held it up to my face. Through the window I could see the mountains, trees below. I perched on the edge of the window and looked to see if there were any other houses near by. Now he was gone I felt I could breathe again and yet, I felt an emptiness, a kind of loss. First my mother, and now him. I pressed my hand against my face to stop the tears from forming. I pulled my shirt straight and checked my clothes, still feeling the heat of his hands pressed against me.

I wandered out of the room onto the landing and leant over the banister to see the hallway below. The house was silent, but I crept down the stairs, watching and listening as I did, for someone or something below. The large door, which led onto the courtyard was closed. I put my hand on the handle and pulled it down, then pushed. The door stood firmly closed. I shook it, in panic, jostling the handle as I did. "No!" I shouted, "He's locked me in!" Then began to laugh as I pushed the handle down again and pulled the door towards me. It opened.

"Idiot," I said aloud. "Why would he lock you in?" I breathed in the scent of the courtyard, jasmine and chickens and ripening fruit and stepped outside. "And why are you talking to yourself?" Satisfied that I was not a prisoner, I turned and went back inside.

Once in the kitchen I set about making coffee in the usual way, taking care to get it right in an effort to dispel that awful feeling of longing for my mother, as if by making coffee exactly as she prescribed I could conjure her up again. I poured the coffee into a thick pottery cup and wandered back into the hallway to find somewhere to sit out of the afternoon heat. The downstairs rooms were dark, windows and shutters closed. One room was furnished as a sitting room, a couch, a low table, a single high-backed chair, an ornately carved wooden table with four heavy chairs at one end. I dropped onto the couch, spilling a little coffee onto my hand. The brief pain was a relief, something real in this still house. I slurped, just like mum did, as Doug did, slurped the hot liquid and drank it down, laughing aloud again as my presence broke the quiet of the place. There was a vase on the table, with a shock of bright pink thrust into it, papery bougainvillea blossoms. I thought it odd that such a neglected room should have this one touch.

They frighten me with tales of brain damage and strangulations, babies starved of oxygen. I am lying in a darkened room, the sounds of other lives outside. A baby's crying. It's hot in here. A high whining of a mosquito with a full belly taunts me. I find it hard to move, the pain comes in waves, every time I do. I close my eyes as the nurse gabbles at me.

"Ponnai," I tell her. IT HURTS. She mutters to her friend and I understand one word, "xeni," foreigners. I try and form the words, WHERE IS MY BABY? But my mind only gives me a nursery rhyme the children in the harbour used to sing.

'Pou'n to, pou'n to, to dachtilithi?' Where is it, where is it, where is the ring?

"Pou'n to?" I manage to ask, "Pou einai to moro mou?" My mouth forms the words against the will of my brain.

"Bay-bee?" The nurse screeches, "Bay-bee sleep now." I lie back with the effort of it all and let my eyes close and when I open them a nurse stands over me, a tiny bundle of white in one hand and a bottle of formula in the other. Her hair is black, dark like those birds and her nose is sharp like a beak.

"Bay-bee eat now," she thrusts the bundle at me and then slams the bottle on the bedside table. I pull myself onto one elbow and shift myself up the bed, the pain across my abdomen stabs as if my guts are about to spill. The bundle makes a tiny mewling sound and I look down to see a tiny red face with a slight golden fuzz across the scalp. She screws her little nose up and opens her mouth to let out a terrifying wail. I pull my nightdress open and manage to latch her on and as her tiny mouth sucks, the pain in my belly stabs again. Each suck pulls at my gut, but she looks up at me and fixes her gaze on mine, and I lie back and let her do her worst.

The sharp-nosed nurse barges in and tuts to see the bottle

rejected on the side, she stands and watches the clock, sighs and leaves again, snatching the bottle as she goes.

I sleep, she feeds, I sleep, she feeds. I sleep. I wake to see Korakas sitting in the chair at my side, Alithea is lying on his chest, her tiny hands out of the tight swaddling grasping his shirt, her eyes closed, his eyes closed, her breathing double time to his as both dream about each other.

"Anna," he smiles at me. His face is as creased as the clothes he's wearing. His dark eyes are shaded underneath, with black rings. His hair falls away from his face. The ache in my belly creeps up to my chest and into my throat and I begin to cry, quietly.

"Annoula-mou, don't cry. They had to cut you for the baby, they had to keep the baby safe. Look how beautiful she is." He holds her up to me, scarcely filling both his hands. He lays her in my arms and touches her face.

"My beautiful daughter, my beautiful wife."

When I wake again two nurses stand over me, the sharp one from before, and a fat one, a shuffler like Chrissoula. They speak but I have no idea what they say. They take me by the arms and swing my legs over the edge of the bed. The pain cuts across my belly again and I cry out. The fat one grumbles at me and slaps her hands in desperation against her thighs which are straining against the fabric of her white uniform. Behind her, standing in the doorway I see Alison, a head taller than either of the women, her hair a blazing halo, the sun streaming in around her. Like some vengeful angel she spits out a stream of incantations and sends them scurrying away from me.

"What on earth did you say to them?"

"I just asked if they'd ever had their bellies split open and a baby yanked out, and if not how did they know whether it hurt or not, because it bloody well does and that they should be careful because if they weren't afraid of me, then at least they should watch out for your husband."

"I've missed you."

"And I've missed you too, you clever, clever girl." She leans forward and kisses me, holds me for a moment, squeezing the breath

194

out of me.

"I've seen her and she's beautiful."

"Where is she?"

"In the nursery downstairs, they've got them lined up in little plastic boxes next to each other!"

"Boxes?"

"You know those plastic bassinet things, little cots on wheels."

"Oh. Did they tell you which one she is?"

"No need, the rest are like little monkeys with black hair all over the place and she's a little pink angel with a golden head!"

"You're the angel, coming in here and putting the fear of God into them."

"They say you need to get up, move around, it helps you heal. Now, lean on me, put your hands across the scar and press. Hold it in. You think it'll all fall out the minute you move but it won't, trust me. Here." She offers her arm and I lean on her and do as she says.

Her hair smells fresh and her skin smells of coconuts with a hint of something else I don't recognise. Slowly I begin to walk, as she encourages me.

"None of that shuffling, stand up straight, it makes it easier."

"How do you know all this?"

"Told you, I've been reading up on it for you."

"It still feels like I'm going to come undone."

"Well you're not."

"How do you know? Just because some bloody mag says so?"

"No, because, oh doubting one, I had a bit of surgery myself a while back, cutting and poking and prodding things about. It's sore for a while because they pull you about, but it'll ease off."

I walk to the door and back a few times, stretching my legs, trying to do as I'm told, then sit on the edge of the bed again, weary. I look up as I hear voices outside. The fat nurse and a man. He snaps at her, she quietens and I hear her shoes squeaking away. Then he's with us in the room, his eyes dark, flicking this way and that, his

195

mouth down turned. He touches Alison's arm, so quickly I'm not even sure if he did or if I imagined it.

"Thank you. I have spoken myself to the nurse. Thank you." Then he comes to me smiling and takes my hands in his to kiss them.

"Brave Anna, they will not trouble you like this, I will take you home. I will care for you," he turns to include Alison, "your friends will help you, we have no need of these foolish islanders. We xeni will take care of our own." Alison's mouth drops open again and I laugh.

"You see what care he takes of me?"

"Yes," she says, "incredible. Absolutely incredible."

The other rooms were empty, so I ventured back upstairs again. The upper floor extended left and right of the stairs and I turned to walk towards the doors I hadn't noticed before. The first room had a small bed in it with a striped blanket flung across it, like the ones I'd seen in the tourist shops in town. I walked to the window, opened it and threw back the shutters to look outside. Below me was a narrow pathway which lead to a grove of trees, beyond this was what looked like the wall of another house.

The next room was empty but for an old trunk and some packing cases. I lifted the lid of one of the boxes and looked inside to find books and papers. I pulled out a sheaf of papers and looked through them. I recognised the symbols and letters on some, but on others the words seemed more like codes and diagrams. Some were intricate drawings, some sketches. The books were old and dusty, tattered covers with damaged corners. I pulled out a roll of paper, slipped off the band which held it tight and gently unfurled it. Broad charcoal streaks showing a man, almost a man, standing, arms stretched wide as if he were about to take flight. His face was hard, his eyes small and round, a bird, not a man at all. The style of the drawing was so reminiscent of those paintings my mother used to do, during those awful spells of solitude. Dark paintings which rarely sold and lay about the house like brooding watchmen. I dropped the drawing, forcing myself to forget the similarity and turned to look in another box. Here were blankets and covers, faded colours, sun streaked by years of use. I plunged my hand deeper and felt something soft, I pulled it towards me and held it up, a dirty, soft toy with a tatty ribbon around its neck, ears bent over, chewed or sucked by a long-forgotten child.

I made my way back down the stairs, the toy still in my

hand. I paused at the door to one of the downstairs rooms and opened it, No hint of how the room may have been used remained, empty of furnishings, shutters closed, the sun casting that striped pattern on to the bare floor. I touched the little toy, closed the door and went back outside.

I walked around the side of the house to try and find the pathway I had seen from the upstairs window, something driving me to discover what lay beyond this house. Its silence, which had seemed so restful, unnerved me now. The chickens clucked and fussed around me and I shooed them out of the way. The pathway ran along the side of the house and gave way to a tree-lined avenue which lead to a crumbling wall. Beyond this were derelict buildings and remnants of what must have been a farm or market garden. Torn plastic sheeting hung from the frame of a poly-tunnel and flapped in the breeze. I shivered, childish thoughts of ghosts and ghouls in my head, and turned to look back at the house. As I did the little toy dropped to the floor from where I had stuffed it into my waistband. I stooped to pick it up again and held it to my face, inhaling as if I could learn its history from its scent. As I stood up again, I noticed a small shed set back from the path in the trees.

"Come on then," I said to the toy, taking courage from its company, "shall we take a look?" Clutching it to me like a talisman, I made my way through the trees, glancing back, sensing something behind me, sounds of the ripped plastic sheeting fluttering, a call from a bird. I began to run.

The shed was built of rough stone, the wooden door hung on one hinge and the roof had tiles missing. The darkness inside was broken by shards of light cutting through the gaps in the roof. The musky odour of goat filled my nostrils, not unpleasant, mixed with the earthy smell of the well-trodden soil which made the floor. I righted a small stool and sat on it, looking out of the doorway. In the corner were ashes from an old fire. I wondered who would have sat in here, so close to the house and that other farm. A noise outside startled me and I leaped up, knocking the stool over again.

"Sorry, sorry! Don't be frightened!" A tall, skinny man appeared at the doorway. He stepped forward and I stepped back.

"Sorry, please, I won't hurt you." He held his hand out to me and stepped a little closer. I swallowed and clutched involuntarily at the toy at my side. The man's eyes followed the movement of my hand and he smiled.

"That's Bunny." I pulled the dirty thing from my waist and studied it,

"Bunny?"

"It was yours, when you was little. Your mum left it when she took you away." He smiled again, "I helped." He stepped closer and the odour of earth and stale sweat jolted my memory. The lilt of his voice reminded me of England, West Country, a comforting sound here where I felt so out of place.

"On a motorbike," I whispered.

"On a motorbike," he nodded eagerly, then stretched out his hand as if to shake mine and added, "Andy."

"You knew us, knew my mother?"

"This was my farm," he grinned, showing an array of discoloured teeth, "well, I worked it. Flowers. We grew flowers."

"Oh," I was unsure how to proceed.

"I seen her, your mum. I seen her here, few days ago." I felt bile rising to my mouth, I swallowed hard. My face was hot and I stretched a hand out to steady myself. Andy caught hold of it and stepped closer to me. The proximity of him made the sickness worse. I fought with the desire to push him away but knew that I would fall if I didn't lean against him, and when I did, the smell of him seemed to fall away and leave just a tall man looking down at me, willing me to be strong. At last someone else believed that my mum was here.

"I found something." He settled me back on the stool and rummaged in an old box which lay in the shadows by the far wall. He pulled out a piece of sackcloth and slowly unwrapped what was inside. "See?" He offered me a small book which had been carefully wrapped and hidden. I took it and thumbed through the pages, recognising the shapes of letters, the curve of an 'e' or the slant of an 'm'. Familiar language in a familiar voice. I leafed through the pages reading a passage or a line

- *I've always been afraid of the dark. But here I am in a*

strange place, the village tucked up for the night, walking to the beach -

I dropped the book from my face and looked up at Andy

- I swing round, my heart swollen to twice its normal size inside my chest, and I will it not to beat. I'm not so afraid once I can see it is a man and not some mythological monster from beneath the sand dunes. -

Leafing through the book I stopped again.

- A rush of wind comes up the alley and almost pushes me over, the noise is like the sea crashing onto rocks. I steady myself against the damp wall and turn to see Korakas. He stands tall, blocking the feeble light from the houses on the street. He has his arms raised, as I had done and he is screeching at them. His eyes are alight, his hair is flying in the strange wind and his features seem angular -

I thought of the charcoal drawing I had dropped back in the house, remembered Doug telling me about his near beating in the harbour all those years ago.

"What is it?" Andy knelt at my feet, "What's wrong?"

"This is my mother's book, from before."

"She left it here when he came for her." I lifted my head to look at him.

"You saw her with this? What do you mean came for her?" I felt my voice waver and stood up, then pushed past Andy to get outside. He ran after me.

"They was rowing a lot, she was crying. She came running down here into my old shed and sat and cried a bit."

"When was this? Did you speak to her?"

"I dunno," Andy shook his head slowly, "days don't always follow for me, d'you know what I mean?"

"Please," I touched his arm, "please, did she talk to you?"

"First off I reckoned I was seeing things. She went a long time ago, you was what, two or three? I saw her down back there," he pointed towards the house.

"She was feeding the chickens just like she'd never been away, she stood up straight and looked towards me, put her hand up, to stop the sun from her eyes. I waved at her, but she didn't do nothing, just bent on down and carried on with them chickens."

I sighed, "so you didn't speak to her?"

"Nah, then he come out, calling for her, she went running, like she always did, like she hadn't seen him for days, hugging him and they kissed just like before when he first brung her up here, but she was crying and he gets angry. Then them bloody birds sees me and calls out to him," Andy gestured to the trees, waving his arms wildly. "Then he sees me and shouts at me, 'Fige!' Like he does, like I'm a dog. And she doesn't look up, just holds on to him like she'll fall down if she don't."

"He came out? Who? Who do you mean?"

"Korakas, your dad."

My mouth went dry, I tried to swallow. "My dad was here?"

"And your mum. That's what I'm saying. I saw her, bit older but I'd know her, still lovely. Then she was here in my shed, few days after that, I heard her shouting and him shouting, then she comes running down here and into my shed. I kept away, didn't want to scare her. She had that book," he touched the book in my hands.

"When she come out she didn't have it no more. So when they was gone I looked and I found it."

"Did you read it?"

"No I can't read it!"

"Oh I'm sorry," I blushed, "I didn't know you couldn't.."

"I can bloody read, but it ain't mine to read is it? But I reckon it's for you, now she's run off like that."

"I'm sorry," I dropped my head and turned the book over in my hands, "it's just, I thought.."

"I know. I seem a bit slow. Keeps people off my back!" He chuckled. I turned the book over again, stroking it, before opening it again.

- *"Where can you tell me, have you been?" His face is dark, his eyes narrow and lose their light. His speech is raw and deep.*

"Well?" Snatching Alithea he pushes past me into the house. Startled, she starts to wail.

"For God's Sake! What's the matter with you?" I shout.

"With me? I ask again, where have you been?" As he paces, his voice grows coarser, until I can hardly make out words. He is spitting words in some strange dialect, cawing and screeching.

"Please, what is it?" I plead. Alithea's cries grow more insistent. I prise her from him and hold her close. "What's wrong with you? You're scaring her. You're scaring me!"

"What kind of mother are you? Just look at yourself! Dressed up like a whore!"

I am holding Ally on my hip, her face is smeared with chocolate from the rich birthday cake she crammed into her mouth minutes ago. She tenses in my arms. We had been laughing and singing in the car on the way home and now all that joy has been snatched from us both in a second. I look down at my dress, stained with juice spilled by one of the kids at the party, at Alithea, sticky, warm, smelling of sugar and skin. He steps forward and wipes his thumb roughly across my lips, his nail catching the side of my face.

"What's this stuff on your face? Who are you trying to impress dressed like this? Look at yourself!" He screams at me, his face contorted, the features beginning to change. I tighten my grip on Ally. She makes me brave and I hold her to me.

"I am looking at myself and do you know what I see?" I am shouting at him now. The black birds in the tree cry out and fly off like a dark cloud.

"Do you know what I see?" I ask him. He seems to grow in stature, his arms held away from his body, as if poised for flight. He darts a look at the trees, then back to me, his eyes small and black now, his face hardened into furrows, but remains silent. So I continue.

"I see a mother and her daughter, come home from a day with friends. Where do you think I've been? Fucking some barman in town with my daughter in tow?"

"Don't speak these words to me!" He raises his hands above his head, blocking out the sun, his transformation complete. A stray feather falls to the floor and lays at my feet. I throw my arm around Ally's head to shield her from him and run inside the house. I turn at the door and cry out, "you've ruined it all, again! You've ruined

202

another lovely day! I hate you!"

I look back and see Korakas sat on the steps, his head in his hands, human, defeated -

I closed the book again, and turned to Andy.

"Can you remember what they rowed about, can you remember anything they said?" He shuffled slightly and looked down at his feet.

"I don't stand around spying you know?"

"I know, but I need to know what's been going on."

"She's been here a couple of days I reckon, a week? I dunno. They been like old times, when they first met, when everybody tried to warn her off him and she wouldn't listen. Then he left her a while, went into town, but left them black birds like he does, watching her. I don't like those birds," he was mumbling half to himself. "You don't see 'em nowhere else, just where he's been about." He looked at me, focussing on me again. "So he leaves her up here, then they had a fight and she went running off. I know you been up here before, with him."

"Where does he fit in to all this? Xenon, where does he fit in?" Andy threw his head back and laughed, "Xenon! That's a laugh. Is that what he calls himself these days?"

"What do you mean, do you know him?"

"Oh girly! I've known him years and years! But he never changes! Didn't you get told not to trust a man out here? Didn't you get told that a man's not always what he seems to be? Eh? Didn't you listen when you got told the tales about this place?"

I drew in my breath noisily, "stories is all I ever got told about this place,"

"And for good reason!"

"I'm sick of you all, Doug and Alison, and now you. You're all crazy, it's no wonder my mother went mad out here." Andy lowered his voice and held me by the arm.

"Now you listen here, your mum weren't never mad and ain't mad now. I'm telling you she was here, she was upset, but she ain't mad."

"Then tell me what you heard and stop the village idiot act!" Andy pulled his hand off my arm as if he'd been scalded.

"Well, like I say, a couple of days ago, maybe a week or so, I see your mum here. Going about her business like she used to. At first they was all lovey-dovey, but then it all changed." I stood quietly as Andy painstakingly related what he had witnessed over the past few days. He spoke as if recounting the events to a court, standing straight, arms by his sides. Concentrating, remembering the details, he continued.

"Your mum, she was down here, tears and all on her face. She was in my shed a while, then I heard him calling her and she goes running out, wiping her face with her hands.

- Anna? - he's calling,

- Come, we have to go.

- Go where? – she says, her voice shaking.

- Town, my house in town.

But she's shaking her head at him.

- I don't want to go - she says - I want to stay here.

But he's holding her and talking like he does, firm but quiet, persuading her, but telling her like she hasn't got a choice, you know? Then he takes her arm and walks her to the truck."

I waited expectantly, before prompting him for more, "and then?"

"I ain't seen your mum no more. Next thing I know, you're up here." I began to walk back towards the house.

"I can't believe I was so close to finding my mother. I knew she'd come here. Do you know where the house is in I town?"

"Not really. But I'll take you in if you like."

"Please." I felt suddenly tired.

"Give me a few minutes, I'll see if I can get the truck, don't reckon we'd make it on my old moped."

As Andy ambled away down the track, I sank to the ground and sat, my back against one of the trees which gave some shade, and turned the pages of my mother's journal.

- At last I'm home. The place looks pretty much the same, chickens in the yard, stores in the apothiki, the paint's peeled a bit more here and there. I take a handful of grain from the tub in the corner and throw it to the chickens, talking to them like I used to. I hear something and look up, the sun is in my eyes, so I hold my hand up and look ahead, but there's nobody there. I turn back to the clucking hens and throw another handful of corn.

"Anna?" My body knows he is calling before my ears hear the sound. I feel a rush of warmth and turn to see him, in the doorway, dark as ever, older, a little grey in his hair, his face lined with the lost years. I run to him and hold him, burying my face in his chest, breathing in that familiar scent, the chill of a winter day, clean air, earth, lemons, olives, the sun, the salt of the sea. I close my eyes and I feel the loss he has felt for the past years. My chest is tight and I'm crying, clinging to him.

"I'm sorry, I'm sorry. I'm home now!"

He wraps his arms around me and enfolds me, kisses the top of my head, pushes me away slightly, then kisses me on the mouth, hard.

"Anna, my Anna." But then I feel his body tense. His face tightens, the lines across his forehead deepen and his eyes shrink to small black beads.

"It is Alithea I need - my daughter."

"Please, that's why I've come," I plead with him, desperate to keep that feeling between us, but he changes so rapidly, I'm losing him. "Please, I'm here, let her go!"

"You fool! You think I want you? I want my daughter! MY daughter!" The birds in the trees call out to him and he waves an arm at them, "FIGE!" He shouts. He is staring towards the old flower farm and waves his arm again. I cling to him, I know I will fall if he lets me go. He turns to look at me, his arm still supporting me. When he looks into my face I know he still loves me.

"Anna," softer now, "Anna, you know that I need her, you must bring her to me." I'm crying, my eyes are sore and my nose runs into my mouth as I speak,

"But I'm here now, we can be happy." He pulls me to him, putting a finger to my lips to quiet me and kisses me again. Then, *holding the weight of me, he walks with me into the house.*

Inside it's dark. The shutters are closed, the air still, the sounds from outside muted. He leads me through the kitchen to the room where we used to sit as a family, the furniture has gone and in its place there are packing cases, filled with memories. He pulls a small blanket from one and holds it up to me.

"Remember when we brought her home from the clinic?" He holds it up to my face and I breathe in. The fabric is soft and I brush it against my cheek.

"I was the happiest man, my wife, my daughter, all that I could ask for."

"I'm sorry, you know I couldn't keep her here."

"But you could, you should have. She is my daughter and to take her from me was unforgivable. How could you?"

"I'm sorry." I whisper the words, because I'm afraid that he'll change into that thing that used to terrify me, sharp, dark, screeching. "I'm sorry." I throw my arms around his neck and plead again, "I'm here. I'll stay with you. You don't need her. I'll stay with you, forever. I swear." I touch his face and wipe a tear from his cheek. His skin is rough, he looks tired, sad, and I know that I've caused it all. He falls onto his knees at my feet and throws back his head, tears fall across his face and onto the tiled floor.

"You know how it has to be! If it could be otherwise I swear I would make it so! But you of all people know!" I drop to the floor in front of him and hold him in my arms. He leans against me, his eyes closed and his breathing slows. He lays his head in my lap and I sit cradling him like my own son, stroking his hair.

For three days we live as we used to, I make him coffee, he cooks for me, we sleep together in our old bed in the bedroom which over looks the courtyard. I wake to sounds of chickens, the scent of jasmine from outside the window. In the afternoon we lie and listen to cicadas singing in the trees. This morning I wake and he's gone. I lean on the window and look outside, the courtyard, the trees, the mountains beyond, snow still on the highest peak. I look back to the room behind me, the white walls, simple furniture, the bed where we have lain for so many hours. I wander out onto the landing and look across towards the stairs. Something catches my eye, caught in a gap between the floorboards. I bend down to pick it up and hold it up to the light, a bracelet with tiny glass beads, each one a different shade of blue, suspended from irregular shaped links, some silver, some gold. They remind me of the ring I wear. I twist it on my finger. A ring which has two counterparts, a silver one which Alithea wears around her neck on a chain and another golden one, yellow gold, not like mine, which he wears around his neck. Three parts of the same piece, a ring his mother gave to him he said. A ring which would bind us together forever. The light catches the beads, sending a tiny blue shaft of light across my hand and I remember Alithea's excitement on her birthday, which seems so long ago. How pleased she was with all her gifts.

"NO!" I cry out loud.

And now it's clear to me what a fool I've been. He has lured me here with his tricks, the gifts at the house, the scarf he sent Alithea, those damn birds telling him where we were and what we were doing every step of the way. And my coming here to beg him to leave her be, has brought her close behind. Of course she was bound to follow, she was bound to know where I'd gone. Why couldn't I control my panic and play clever? He always could control every move, knew what I'd do, how I'd react and like a fool I've lead her right to him. And if she's been here, how can I know what's already happened, if I'm too late? I'd rather die than have her harmed by him.

I leave the house and find my way down the old path to Andy's farm. I keep my head down, the tears are stinging my face. I can't let those birds see me. I begin to run. I make my way to the old shed. The air inside is heavy with the smell of goats and musty earth. I sit inside and let the tears fall. My old journal is still safely wrapped in its hiding place where I left it a few days before. It protects my thoughts from him. He finds his way inside my head, but my most private thoughts are safe on these pages. Writing clears my head and leaves nothing behind for him to find. He'll never know what I intend next.

I know at last what I must do. As long as I am here Ally will look for me. I thought I could persuade him to let her go. If I'm gone *she'll go back home, it's just the search for me that keeps her here. Doug and Alison will make sure she gets away. The loss of me will be shock enough to send her home and if she goes home he won't be able to fetch her back again, he doesn't have that power.*

There is a beach where we used to go, near the village. The sand is fine and pale, the waves pull across the bay and cause a rip, an undertow. I've seen people swim out, playing in the surf, then panic as it catches them. I saw one girl, slipped off her bright pink lilo. We were on the shore, oblivious to her struggle. One of the boys swam out to her. We were laughing at their horseplay in the water, jumping and diving in the waves, clutching the water-bed as it bobbed up and down, his arms around her, her arms around his neck. Then when they re-joined us we saw her face, she'd thought she was going to drown.

I lay the bracelet between the pages of my journal and start to wrap up the book, but then change my mind. I miss Ally so badly. I push the bracelet deep into my pocket. To have a little piece of her with me will be a comfort. I push the little book back into the box where I know it will be safe.

I let the book close and clutched at my wrist, realising that my bracelet was no longer there. I began to run towards the old farm, words crashing inside my head - I would rather die - I know at last what I must do – there is a beach where we used to go.
A hunched figure on a rusty motorbike appeared at the end of the track, Andy grinning, astride it. He stopped as I ran to meet him.

"The village," I panted, "what village? Do you know?" I thrust the book at Andy, "I would rather die, she says! There is a beach near the village, with a bad current, an undertow!"

"I know where she used to work, there is a beach out that way, no good for swimming."

"I would rather die, she says!" My voice grew shrill.

"Shh, quiet. I can't take you all the way out there on this," he pointed at the battered old moped, "I couldn't get the truck."

I was crying now, "you must, you have to, please."

The beach stretched out before Anna, couples lay on towels, girls chatting down by the waves, which lapped at the sand, the sound restful. A few metres out, the waves broke, white surf against the blue green sea. The sun was beating down and she felt the pleasurable sensation of her skin tightening. She slipped her sandals off as she walked, first one and then the other, leaving them behind like footprints. She unfastened her skirt and let it drop onto the sand, stepped out of it and continued towards the sea. All she could hear was the sound of the waves - shh, shh - singing to her - shh, shh – calming her.

In her mind she went over the words she had written to her oldest friends

- *Alison, look after Alithea, tell her your truth, about her father, and she will not seek him out, she will know he has nothing for her. I am sorry, but with me gone she will be free and he can never harm her. My lovely Doug, please know that you are the one I trust with my baby's safety, but for her sake you must not perpetuate that awful myth, instead let Alison fill her head with tales of a man, a powerful, controlling man, but just a man. I know you will always give her a home in your lovely English house. Please know I have thought this through and through. If I do this she will be safe, believe me deluded, and let me go, leave this place and keep far away from him. She knows how much I love her, but tell her that this island and her father drove me to it. Please let the stories rest with me -*

The water lapped around her ankles, cooling her feet, hot from the sand. She heard a girl call out to a friend, a child laughing, the sea whispering – shh – shh. She waded further out and felt the spray as it wet her face, tasted the salt, like tears. She lay herself down and let the water wash over her, felt the tug at her feet. For a second she tried to stand, but was knocked back by the waves. Her mouth filled with water and she gagged, coughing, fighting, despite herself, to lift her head to take a breath.

Suddenly she felt fingers grip tightly around her wrist. Through her streaming eyes she saw him, Korakas. He pulled her close, holding her around the waist. Lifting her higher as a new wave swept up and over them both. Together they fell, were pulled as the grip of the sea took them under the surface. She felt his grip loosen, she felt herself being pulled away again, then his hand grasped hers, slipped and grasped her wrist again. He lifted her arm high, a parody of a dance, while the people on the beach went about their business. She felt the strength of him and willed herself to drag her body back towards the shore, just to be with him again, just to hear his voice, feel his breath on her. She felt her feet touch sand, then stumbled, found footing again. He was pushing her, dragging her, then together they fell onto the shore, the sea lapping now, gently, around them. He pulled her towards him and wrapped his arms around her.

"I should have let you drown!" She was shivering, her skin hot, but shock gripping her by the throat.

"Then why didn't you?" She coughed, tears filling her eyes.

"What is my life without you?" He whispered into her hair.

"I can't let you have Alithea."

"Having her gives me my freedom, but what is my freedom without you?"

"But I'll grow old and die."

"I will endure the eternity without you just to have you with me now." She felt her face flush and laughed awkwardly. There he goes talking crap, like old times, she thought and felt young again.

She leant on him as they walked back to his motorbike, like two tourists after a day on the beach. He lay a towel across the seat, then pulled a shawl from the pannier and wrapped it around her shoulders. She held it up to her face and lay her cheek against the soft fibres. As he drove them across the rough track to join the highway, she held tightly to him, breathing in the scent of the shawl and of him, all thoughts of Alithea, of England, gone.

*

The moped struggled along the highway, I sat behind Andy, teeth gritted, willing him to go faster. Finally Andy nodded his head,

"that's the village." He continued driving without saying a word until he turned off the road by a sign which read PARADISE in neon letters.

"Here you go, Paradise!" He chuckled. He coasted the old bike to a standstill. "Jump off!"

I did as I was told and looked past the beach hut which served as a bar, to the sea beyond.

"I need a drink."

"No!" I shouted. Andy started at the sound of my voice.

"I need you! You can't get pissed now!"

"Don't see what I can do. I told you, that's the beach," he nodded his head at the beach and ambled off towards the bar.

The beach here had few people on it, the sea was a deep blue-green and the waves rippled onto the shore. Further out I could see that surf would build up and dissipate before it reached the shore. So used to tides in England I hadn't noticed that the sea on the island beaches generally laps at the shore like the water in a boating pond at the park. This beach, I realised, was deceptively calm, gentle lapping waves, with the tell-tale foam of surf a few metres out. I began to walk along the sand, slipping my shoes off to feel the heat of it between my toes. As I walked I scanned the beach for some sign that my mother had been here. I thought about asking at the bar, but the sight of Andy propping himself up on one elbow, swigging from a bottle, had put me off.

I began to run, the stitch in my side some relief from the aching in my head and that heavy feeling in my chest that had started soon after I had read the journal.

When the stitch became too much, I stopped, bent double, resting my hands on my thighs for support to try and relieve it. As I raised my head again, I caught sight of a sandal, lying in the sand. I walked slowly towards it, bent and picked it up, then scanning around, noticed its partner. Some way beyond was a cloth or a towel, as I bent to pick that up I realised it was a skirt, not just any skirt but my mother's.

I fell to my knees and let out a moan. I curled myself into a ball, clutching my mother's few things to me and sobbed.

My face was tight from the salt of tears and the damp sand from the beach, dried by the sun. I walked slowly back up to the road and jumped on the town bus as it pulled in at the stop. I sat quietly on the slow journey home, holding my mother's shoes, her skirt and the journal, in my lap.

By the time I reached town, the sun was setting over the harbour. I stepped across the low-slung chain which stopped cars from driving through. The bars were full, the restaurants busy, people strolling around the harbourfront, couples arm in arm. I heard the sounds but didn't register which one went with which activity. A waiter called out to me, "ela, messa," inviting me to eat in his restaurant, thrusting a menu at me. I shook my head. Another voice called, I blanked it out, but a hand touched my arm. I looked up to see Costas.

"Miss Alithea?" He pulled me towards the café, held me by the arm and I let him lead me. He spoke quickly, softly, then shouted to his brother, something about a telephone. "Katse," I sat as he had asked, at his table where he usually sat watching the world go by, waiting to take orders.

"Ally, thank God!" I looked up to see Doug running towards me, he squeezed between the tables, knocking against people as he did.

"Ally! We've been so worried." I sat as still as I could, knowing that if I moved, or tried to speak I would unravel completely.

"Ally, honey, let's get you home." He offered his hand, waved to Costas and nodded his thanks. He lead me out of the café, between the tables and walked with my arm linked through his to my hotel.

"What's all this stuff?" He poked at the bundle I was clutching as we walked. I made no reply. "We'll pick up some things and take you back to our house. Then we can talk," he smiled and squeezed my arm, trying to inject some life into me.

At the hotel the receptionist handed me a package with my key and Doug snatched it from her.

"No! You don't need to read all this now."

"What is it?" Finding my voice jolted my mind, "wait a minute, it's the story I found in the library."

"Hon, you don't need this now. We need to talk."

"Give it to me, I'll read it later." We walked around the hotel and turned into the street which lead to the door of my room.

"Al's waiting for you at home, she's made up the couch for you, and we'll get some food inside you."

"Doug, these are my mother's things." I held up the bundle of cloth. Doug unrolled the skirt to find the shoes and the small notebook.

"What do you mean where did you get these?"

"On the beach. She's drowned herself. Look. It says so in here." I held up the journal and Doug took it from me as I put the key in the door and let us into the room. I sank onto the bed, my legs suddenly weak.

"I would rather die, she wrote."

"Ally, honey, we got a letter from her, a note, we didn't know what to do. I've been looking all over for you, we didn't know where to look for her, or if we should go to the police, we didn't know what to do." His voice trailed off and I realised he was crying. Doug shook his head, "I didn't believe she was here."

*

Through the door Alison could see into the room where Ally lay curled up on a bed settee, an old wooden contraption, with a blanket thrown over her.

"Look at her," she whispered to Doug, "She's exhausted,

213

God knows what went on today."

"She seemed pretty shaken, but she wouldn't let me look at that book or take those shoes and clothes off her. Do you think they are Anna's?"

"I don't know, she seemed pretty sure," Alison peered through the gap in the door to watch Ally as they spoke, "I think it's time we went to the police." Doug snorted.

"What d'you think the police will do? A crazy note from a foreigner, a pair of sandals on a beach, what do they care?"

"Well the Consulate then. We should have taken this more seriously before. I just never believed Anna would come back here."

"Go to the Consulate and say what? That we've had a suicide note from a friend we haven't seen in over a decade?"

"Ssh, don't say suicide, she may not be asleep."

"Al honey this is what we're talking about here, if the note came from Anna."

"Of course it came from Anna," Alison caught her breath, "Oh Doug, what's happened to her? We have to get the authorities involved. Suppose some thing's happened to her. Suppose she has hurt herself?"

Doug looked through the doorway at the sleeping girl, so like her mother in the half light. "Do you think Anna would drown herself?"

"I just don't know. What's she got in her hand?" Alison nodded towards Ally.

"Bunny," he replied.

"Bunny? Where did that come from?" Alison peered in to take a closer look.

"She always had it when she was a kid."

"I know that! But Anna left it at the house when they ran away. She thought it would buy them time, if he saw bunny he'd never believe they'd gone far."

"So she's been to the house you think and found it? Do you think he kept it all these years?"

"I don't know, but we have to get some help on this, I don't like any of it and I want to know what's happened to Anna."

The house is quiet except for the occasional sound of a motorbike driving past outside. I have to think for a moment where I am, so many events have happened and I have been to so many places in so few days.

I am in Doug and Alison's house, in the harbour. They have brought me here because my mother is dead and they worry what I'm going to do. When I hear them whispering I know they're still not sure if she came here at all. They're not sure that the clothes I found are hers. But in the pocket I find my bracelet, with the tiny blue beads on it. I remember the day she bought that skirt, should she buy the green one, should she buy the grey one? I remember when she caught her heel in the hem and ripped a hole in it, only weeks after she had bought it. I remember how carefully she stitched it so you could hardly see the tear. Now I can rub my finger across the mend and feel where her fingers held the fabric. I know it's there, I know she stitched it and I know she was wearing this skirt yesterday until she let it drop to the sand and walked into the sea.

I sit up and straighten my clothes. The fluffy toy I found at the house falls onto the floor, so I pick it up and put it on the low table in front of me. My mother's journal is under the pillow where I slept and the envelope the hotel receptionist gave me is on the floor by my side. I slip my shoes on and go out into the hallway. A narrow staircase leads upstairs, I can hear snoring, regular and deep. Doug or Alison? I smile and laugh to myself, but then my head reminds the muscles in my face about the events of the previous day and they check my smile.

Across the hall is a small kitchen. I fill a briki with water and begin the routine of making coffee, stirring the grounds, waiting for the right moment to remove it from the heat, that familiar action brings a wave of nostalgia tinged with grief as I pour the liquid into a cup.

I carry the drink back into the room where I slept and read through the documents in the envelope, sipping the coffee as I do. A copy of the picture of Naucrate, the beautiful slave, is the first thing I see. The resemblance to mum hurts me today. The shape of the brow and something in her eyes, the tilt of her head and the length of her neck. The translation of the myth is not as beautiful as the one I heard in the library. The girl had spoken in such rhythmic language. Doug's version is so like Doug, solid and real. He has added copious notes about myths and legends surrounding the island, about a stranger, half-man half-crow, the vrykolakas, a kind of vampire. There are stories of incest, the labyrinth, strange mechanical contraptions built by Daedalus. He continues the story of Daedalus beyond the death of Icarus, charting his journey to Sicily where he became inventor to the king. How Minos followed intending to kill Daedalus, but was instead killed himself by the king. How Daedalus searched his whole life to seek Naucrate, his true love, but never found her.

There are stories of people who have witnessed incredible events, where the bird man fought to protect the people of the island, during the war, after the war, or had punished those who had crossed him. There were ancient tales handed down from father to son of vendettas and reprisals.

The face in the painting looks up at me from the table, so I turn to mum's journal. I know the feelings she had, I have followed in her steps on this island, I've seen what she saw. I read about the boy who died on Ochi Day, how Korakas stepped in and dealt with it all and then took her to his house. I read for clues, I turn page after page, piecing together a view or a smell, a sound, a street, to try and discover where the house might be. I'm sure that Xenon will be there. Why did he leave me at the house in the mountains? Why did he take me where Korakas took my mother? He is a part of this, he knows what Korakas knows, behaves as he does. Why does he wear my father's ring about his neck? I am frightened that the bond I felt may be due to our blood, what if Korakas had a son? What have I done if Xenon is his son? What have we done?

Closing the front door quietly behind me I walk back through the streets to find the harbour front, as a starting point to my search. As I turn the corner, I find I am near the covered market, where during the day, you can buy fresh fish, meat, cheeses, herbs and spices. An old cross-shaped building which houses all the smells and flavours of the island. The main doors are closed, but a lorry is parked at the side door and a man is unloading boxes of green vegetables, great crates of the things. I step aside to skirt around and hear a voice calling me.

"Oy! Ally love, you alright?"

I turn to see Andy sitting on a bench watching the men unloading their trucks. He grins at me, showing me those awful teeth. I turn away again and walk on.

"Aw, don't be like that." I can hear him lumbering behind me, his feet dragging as he shuffles along the road. "Ally love, don't be like that." I know he won't give up, so I stop and turn to look back at him. I feel all the anger of the last days well up, I feel the heat as my face reddens.

"You pathetic piss head! I needed you!" Then I laugh. "God that feels better!"

"Come on Al, buy us a drink and let's make up."

"I'll buy you a coffee." I tell him.

"Aw, I hate coffee."

We sit outside a small kafeneon, the owner gives me a frosty look. I stare back at him in defiance, but then look down at myself and see that my clothes are as creased and dishevelled as Andy's. Andy sips his coffee noisily, reminding me of mum and that habit she had of slurping the hot coffee. It seems like everywhere I turn there's something to remind me of her. I feel so strongly that she has gone, the loss of her like a presence next to me.

"Andy?"

"Yeah?" He's laughing to himself.

"Do you know where Korakas's house is, in the harbour?" He stops laughing.

"I know where it's near."

"Will you show me?"

"Aw, buy us a drink and I might."

"Take me as close as you can remember and I'll by you a drink once we're there."

"Deal." Leaning against the table he levers himself to his feet. I wave some money at the owner and stick a note under my coffee cup. He throws back his head in recognition, in that way they have out here. I keep a reasonable distance from Andy, that pungent smell is frankly a stink, when you're too close, but I follow him as he weaves his way like a stray dog through the streets.

"It's up by the Thursday market," he calls back to me over his shoulder. We skirt the harbour and climb a slope to the top of the old burial mound, then cross between the cars and begin to walk through residential streets.

"Somewhere round here, I dunno, there's steps up I think, like a courtyard out front. Behind the olive factory, near a square, then the road runs all the way up back to the main road, there's a butcher's shop, used to be a kafeneon." We arrive at a small square and Andy drops into a chair outside a café.

"That's me done." He's pathetic, but he's done more to help me than the rest of them. I chuck some money onto the table and leave him to it. There's no need to thank him, he's already ordering a beer.

I'm walking along a narrow street feeling stupid. My mother is gone and I am chasing a man I know nothing about, except that he makes me feel a part of something. Right now that's what I need. I need Xenon. I feel so ashamed that I should contemplate seeking him out when I should be mourning my mother, but something is spurring me on, drawing me. If only I could feel his arms around me he could stop me from feeling so lost.

I hear a gentle toot on a horn and I step out of the way of a van as it trundles past, then I start back along the street. As the van clears my view, I see him walking ahead of me. He's carrying a loaf of bread, strolling, relaxed. He sways as he walks, swinging the bread. I've never seen him like this before, from a distance. Each time we meet he has been waiting for me, watching, or he just appears at my side. I feel my heart speed up, I want to hear his voice, feel his skin, his hand on me, breathe in his smell. He turns a corner and I run, to catch him, wanting to call out to him, but then he's gone.

Ahead, the street is empty. I'm alone. I've no idea of where he might be and I feel the loss of him far deeper than the loss of my mother. This time it's me drowning. I begin to panic. I'm being swallowed down. I try to hold on to the memory of her, to keep me safe, so that I don't need to find him. If I hold on to her she will hold me up, but I can't see her anymore. I can see the painting of the slave, but her features blur into mine, and then his. I throw my hands out and feel the cold stone of the wall and I feel my way along it, following the way he had been walking. My head is rushing, I can hear my own heart pumping, pumping, my breath is short. I feel along the wall and reach a gap, a gate. I look through it and he's there, climbing a staircase up to a balcony, running along the length of the house.

My breathing steadies, I can hear the sounds of the street again, calls of greeting from neighbour to neighbour, cars, motorbikes. I watch him walk along and let himself in through the front door. Without hesitation I follow him, up the stairs and along the balcony towards the door. The house has several windows along its length, as I pass I look inside to see a kitchen.

A woman is sitting at a table, resting her head in her hands, her hair across her face. The kitchen door opens and I step back to avoid being seen. Then I look again, carefully, quietly. I see a man, dark haired, his face lined, darkened by the sun. He is standing behind the woman with his hands resting on her shoulders, he lifts her hair from her neck and kisses it, then slips his hand down the front of her blouse. She throws her head back and arches her neck and he kisses her again. I feel the pleasure that she feels and hear a sound escape my lips. I put my hand to my mouth, angry, hurt, jealous. I don't know why. The woman laughs, a sound from a long time ago, from my memories. Then I hear his voice, low and soft, as he says something in reply, a voice I know. The woman looks up, tossing her hair aside and glances towards the window and I am looking straight into my mother's eyes. And there we are, my face reflected in the glass, as if we are side by side. I hold up my hand and lay it on the glass, but she stares straight through me. I look at the man and realise it is Xenon, I wonder how I could have mistaken him for anybody else. I hear a sound and realise I have cried out loud. He pulls his hand from my mother's blouse and for a moment we are all three side by side, caught staring in the glass.

I run. I fly back down the stairs and into the street.

"Alithea! Wait!" Footsteps running behind me, then I feel his arm on mine, he swings me round and holds me still. I'm crying.

"Wait, you don't understand." I do understand. Phrases from the myth crashing round in my head. I understand the way he manipulated every meeting, the trips to the mountains, our relationship mirroring my mother's past. Now I understand how he feels so familiar, as if we are one and the same. He pulls me close, I feel him pressing against the length of my body. But I pull away, words and phrases, emotions and explanations jostling for space in my mind. I whisper angrily,

"Naucrate was of noble blood and only her bloodline would set him free." Then I fall back against him, needing to feel his arms around me, unable to hold myself apart.

"You are that bloodline Alithea." When he speaks my name I feel empowered, as if I could achieve anything I set my mind to.

"Alithea, we can be together. I need you, but I love her, don't you see? I have waited my whole life for you, but who could tell that I would fall so much in love with her? We can be together, but just let me have these few years with her, we can be together, all three."

I lift my head to look at him and he bends towards me, I feel excited and appalled but I let him press his lips against mine.

I close my eyes and speak softly to him. I know all the things I should be saying, the things a decent girl should say. But when I speak, I hear acceptance, so I try again.

"She seems so happy. How can I take that from her?"

"But how can you deny me happiness with you? How can you deny your own happiness? I know you want me."

"I do, but I want peace for her." I hear myself speak the words and the old Ally feels shocked that this new Alithea could even begin to consider what he is suggesting.

"And for me Alithea? Will you sentence me to live alone until I meet another such as your mother? What if there is no other Anna? What if I never find freedom? And how can you live a life without me? We were meant to be."

The old Ally pushes him away, but he pulls me to him again sharply, his nails digging into the flesh of my arms,

"and can you walk away from her? Leave her here with me?"

"You're hurting me," I try to pull my arm free.

"I am sorry," he let's me go. "I want to hold you, keep you here but I need you to stay of your own free will."

"And I'm sorry," I touch his face and stroke his cheek, "I can't stay, and yes, I can leave her here. I know you'll keep her safe." I am shaking, I feel weakened. I stand a moment, until I'm certain that I can break away and then turn and walk slowly down the street.

As I walk, I feel my strength flooding back and when I reach the corner I turn to take one last look. I see an old man walking away, slender and dark, his hair shines greenish black, with streaks of grey through it. I watch until he turns into the gate of the house and disappears from sight.

I find my way back to the harbour and stop at a kiosk.

"Telefono?" I ask the man inside. He passes me a telephone and I dial the number carefully. I listen to the ringing tone, far off, wait for it to connect.

"Hello Richard?" I pause.

"I'm coming home." He talks, questions. I wait until he stops. Then I speak again.

"I'm sorry. She's gone. I'll be coming home alone."

About The Author

Anne Holloway grew up in Bath and lived in London before moving to Greece in her mid twenties. She lived on the island of Crete for six years.

Some of this story is based on what she experienced, saw and heard while she lived there, some is based on Greek tales and mythology and some is complete fabrication.

When she returned to England she moved to Nottingham with her two children, where she still lives with her third child.

She studied English at Nottingham Trent University and continued to complete an MA in Creative Writing. The course actively encouraged students to seek publication and the contacts she made there lead her to become involved in the local writing community. It is the support of that community, along with encouragement from friends and family, which has been pivotal in her development.

She launched Big White Shed in 2015 not simply as a small press, but also to cultivate a network of practitioners who offer each other support and advice in getting their work out into the world.

She is a freelance writer, performer and teacher and Professional Development Manager for The Mouthy Poets.

With Thanks To

Robert Lever for artwork, cover design and logo.
Maxine Linnell for editorial advice.
Ruth Marler for research and editorial support.
Dan Radburn for technical support.

Sarah Williams, Elisabeth Geake, Jane-Anne Hodgson for critical reading and encouragement.
To all my impartial readers, including Clare Soar and Hannah Soar.

Suzanne Britten, Sebastian Soar and Lucy Black for market research support.

My friends and BHS girls for encouragement.

Frances Thimann for pointing me towards Naucrate's story.

Mouthy Poets and Nottingham Writers' Studio for providing a creative community.

Tutors and fellow course mates on Nottingham Trent University Creative Writing MA 2005-2007 for pushing me.

Big White Shed has been supported by
Ruth Marler, Stephen Marler, Robert Lever,
Clare Soar, Barry Ryan, Catherine and Andy Hutchison.